THE LEGACY

THE
LEGACY

A NOVEL BY

TREVOR L EVANS

A catalogue record for this book is available from the National Library of Australia

ISBN 978-1-7643953-0-4 (Print)
ISBN 978-1-7643953-1-1 (eBook)

CHAPTER 1

Is it all but a dream looking back on life? What does the future have in store?

Jackie and I have moved into a retirement village in northern Victoria. While we miss our little cottage in the Dandenong Ranges, we have accepted that where we are now is the right place for our retirement.

At the moment we are sitting in our lounge. Jackie is doing her Hardanger embroidery, and I am resting my eyes! I am warm and comfortable, totally relaxed. I am not worrying about the world and feel like I'm floating on air. Suddenly, I heard the front doorbell chime. I looked over to Jackie. She was already getting out of her armchair to go to the front door. I thought it would be one of her sewing friends, but she returned to the lounge with two gentlemen. They were both very well dressed in modern business suits, shiny shoes, and well-groomed hair.

I stood up, and was surprised at how quickly I did so, as normally, I have a few problems in this area.

One of the gentlemen asked if I was Mr Trevor Leslie Evans.

I replied, 'Yes, I am.'

He said, 'I am Mr Faulkner, and this is Mr Taylor.' We shook hands, and I noticed they were both Freemasons.

'How can I help you, gentlemen?'

They grinned at each other. 'May we sit down please, Sir?'

Jackie offered them refreshments, and I asked them to not call me sir, call me Trevor. They raised their eyebrows, and I thought they had surprised looks on their faces.

'Now, gentlemen, how can I help you?'

'Well, Sir, or Trevor, that is a puzzling question because we work for you! Please let us explain. We are company lawyers, and we now work for you. Do you know of a gentleman by the name of Peter Smith?'

'Not that I can recall.'

'Well, Peter Smith owned a large company in England. He has died and has left his entire company to you.'

I thought, is this some sort of joke? Jackie was staring at me with a puzzled look. I know what I was thinking to myself, but the words came out aloud. 'Why would Peter Smith leave me his company?'

'Yes Trevor, that puzzled us as well. For the record, we are aware that you were born in England, your mother died when you were very young and you were placed in a children's home. Your father later remarried and brought you to Australia when you were fifteen years old. You went to live in Orbost in Gippsland, where you worked on a dairy farm for three years before working in a sawmill for nine months, and then on a fishing trawler for a year. On your return to Melbourne, you worked as a rigger and then a crane operator until your retirement. You didn't fully retire though as you became involved in the spiritual world. Your mind works differently from a lot of other people, which is why we believe Peter Smith has left you his company. We also know that your wife, Jackie, has been a great part of your success. They both slightly bowed their heads to her, in respect.

'We also know your past employers respected you for your honesty, integrity, and ethics. You made them money.'

'Have you left me with any secrets?' I asked.

'I believe we all have secrets that those above us in the organisation need. May I say they are a bit concerned.'

My thoughts went to the glass brick that I had in my workshop! I keep it to remind myself just how gullible I can be. The joke was on me now. I sat there staring at the two gentlemen, thinking of everything they said. It certainly wasn't April Fool's Day!

'So, you want us to go to England?'

'Yes Sir.' A grin came over his face. 'Sir, I mean, Trevor.'

I liked him; he had a sense of humour.

'When?'

'Today!'

I looked at Jackie. She hesitated for a moment. 'I cannot leave Jackie, Charlie, and the family.' Charlie had heard his name and was wagging his tail.

'Trevor, we have your private aircraft waiting for you at the local airport.'

My private plane? This was becoming more confusing. I always used humour to control my mind. All I had ever wanted was an MG Classic two-seater soft top car.

Jackie's voice broke my thoughts. 'If you put on a suit, I will pack some things in a bag for you.'

The decision had been made!

I went and put on a suit. I was sitting on the bed fully dressed, and Jackie walked in and sat down alongside me. I looked straight into her eyes.' What's happening Jackie? Is this a dream?'

'Trevor, I think you must go with the flow and see where it leads. If you want me, I will follow you when I have sorted out everything here.'

'I will miss you, Jackie. I will be lost without you. I said that I wouldn't leave you again, and here I am, leaving for England! I feel lost and totally confused. There are too many questions and no answers.'

We stood up and embraced each other and said, with sadness, our goodbyes.

'Charlie, you look after your mum!' He just sat there, wagging his tail.

Before I realised it, I was sitting in an aircraft with beautiful leather seats. I should say armchairs. I clipped up my seat belt.

CHAPTER 2

I glanced out of the window, watching the ground disappear from beneath us.

I had flown many times before, but never like this. In what seemed like seconds, we were up in the air, climbing rapidly and before I could even blink, the aircraft had levelled out.

A flight attendant appeared out of nowhere. 'Can I get you a drink, Sir?'

'Yes, please. Make it a double scotch and dry ginger please, one piece of ice only.'

She soon returned with the drink and said with a smile. 'Not stirred Sir!'

I looked up into her eyes and saw her cheeky grin. I felt frozen in time for a moment. Those were the eyes of Michelle, my niece, who had died some years ago.

The flight attendant turned around and went back to her galley, leaving me frozen in time. I shook myself, picked up my scotch and dry ginger, and swallowed two mouthfuls quickly. This was a good-quality scotch. Am I in a dream? No, everything seemed to be real. The flight attendant returned with some food, and there was a plate of honey prawns. She put them down in front of me with a napkin and went back to her galley. How did she know that my favourite food was honey prawns? She then returned with a bowl of peas and creamed mashed potatoes and left.

I looked at the two lawyers sitting with me, trying to think what questions to ask, but there were too many racing through my mind. I felt a sense of fear of what was happening, and then I remembered an old friend's words. *"A man who runs from his fears is out of control, but a man who stands and faces them is in control of them."*

'Gentlemen, I have a lot of questions with no answers. Could you please talk to me about the company? Not the nitty-gritty, just the basics and I will listen.'

They looked at each other. 'First of all, my name is Bill; my colleague is Frank. We first started with the company some twenty-five years ago; we started at the very bottom. Peter Smith spoke to us and said that we were both very intelligent young lads, and if he put us through college and we got our law degrees, we could come back and work for him. He advised that the company would employ us when we were studying during our breaks from college. The one thing that he asked of us was that we were loyal to him and his company. We shook hands and confirmed his wishes. The man who calls himself the General Manager is Mr Neil Gilham. If you were to ask us what we thought of him, well, he is the school bully. In respect to Peter Smith, we do as he asks. We don't necessarily like it. Now though, we work for you and we will do as you ask instead.'

'So, Neil Gilham's wife is also his business partner and is the biggest problem in the company. She has no tact or understanding and she has no compassion for others. She is the most disliked person in the organisation.

'Peter Smith's office, or should I say your office, is exactly as he left it. Nobody has used it, because legally it is your office. We would suggest to you that the first thing you do when you get to the office is you make sure Ms Chris Ayres is hired as your secretary. She was Peter Smith's right hand, and Mrs Gilham wants her gone.

'When Peter Smith could not manage the company because of illness with cancer, Mr Gilham arranged a partnership with a company in Dubai, to build a skyscraper alongside yours. If I could describe the building, it would look like a big Huntsman trumpet or a Coachman's horn. It would be thirteen stories higher than your building. Now we do not know for sure, but talking to a good colleague outside the company has let us know that Mr Gilham wants to float the company on the market as a public company, relying on the shares for money.

'Mr Smith has business arrangements that Mr Gilham does not know about, though, especially with people who have helped him climb the ladder. Good friends. There is one of these friends in Singapore who wishes to talk with you. We have arranged for him to meet you on this trip, if you wish. Mr Gilham has advised us to just refuel in Singapore and leave as soon as we have refuelled, but I believe, by law, the crew on this aircraft need a break as well,' he said with a grin.

I nodded to Bill and grinned. I need a break as well.

'So, you could meet him on this plane in private.'

I thought nothing ventured, nothing gained. 'Yes, Frank.' I took a deep breath and said, thank God that it had already been arranged.

'When we arrive in Dubai, we are supposed to refuel again and depart straight away, but with your permission we have already arranged another meeting for certain people who want to talk to you there as well. Again, we have arranged for this meeting to be held onboard this plane so that no-one knows of this meeting either.'

'Now gentlemen, I have enough in my mind just now. I think we need another drink. The flight attendant brought three drinks and a small tray of egg sandwiches.

I said to the flight attendant, 'There is a good friend of mine in Australia who would be scowling at me if he knew I was eating egg sandwiches.'

I also thought we were going to have secret meetings, but this flight attendant would know everything.

Frank interrupted my thoughts. 'Trevor, could I introduce you to Mr Smith's granddaughter? She is our flight attendant and is training to become an airplane pilot. Her name is Michelle.'

I had that odd feeling inside again. I must control it. I stood up and shook her hand. 'It looks like I'll have a big job to do for your granddad. I know that I'm going to need your help. Please get yourself a drink and come and sit with us. We are family.'

'Thank you, Sir.'

'No, my name is Trevor to you.'

I sat back down and took a sip of my drink, closed my eyes and went through all the major points in my mind about our previous conversation. After a while, I opened my eyes and thought, egg sandwiches and reached out and took two. I said to myself. 'Good luck to you, Mr Harrison, they're all mine!'

I now thought of Jackie. What would she think about this mess? With what I now know, do I have the trump card? I think so.

'Michelle, the gentlemen here tell me I own everything. Has your grandfather set up you financially?'

'Yes, he has. My grandfather had many different projects set up with various friends. He has left me with those little projects to manage myself and then divide the profits equally between me and his friends. With your permission, could these two gentlemen look after my interests? I will pay them.'

'Michelle, these two gentlemen work for your grandfather's company, so they work for you too, in the company's time, and I will pay them.' I looked at her seriously.

She grinned at me. 'My grandfather always said we are talking money, and the money is in my interest. I will not argue with you.'

'Michelle, what sort of chess player has your grandfather left me with?' The two lawyers grinned.

My mind was ticking over. Could Peter have left the company to Michelle? No, she is too young. Although she is intelligent, she is not streetwise yet. She would have to be cruel and hard to make the company survive. I believe she has the standards and ethics which will do her well in the future, but for her, this is the wrong time to have such a burden.

I reached out and took two more egg sandwiches and drank my scotch. I sat there staring out of the window, trying to clear my mind.

The lawyers had advised me of the personalities of my Manager, Neil Gilham, and my Senior Sales Manager, Neil's wife. Why would Peter hire these people? Are they born into the upper circle of society, where he couldn't go? Peter's right hand, Chris Ayres; I needed her and her loyalty to Peter and the company. Peter's friend in Singapore, they have been waiting five years or more for a decision! The skyscraper was shaped like a huntsman trumpet and thirteen stories higher than mine! Another private meeting, or is it a secret meeting? Neil Gilham doesn't want me to talk to anyone? Michelle is Peter's granddaughter, so I think he would want me to protect her at all costs. I chuckled. If I can't swim, how do I protect another person so important to Peter? And where are Michelle's parents?

I was still looking through the window, watching the clouds float by. The two young lawyers gave me a sense of security, and they were also the key to what I needed. I think you have set this up well, Peter! I felt a hand on my right shoulder. I turned around expecting to see someone, but there wasn't anyone. I smiled. I'm not alone. Peter is here.

CHAPTER 3

I must have fallen into a deep sleep when I heard Michelle's voice. 'Trevor, Trevor, we will be landing in Singapore shortly. Would you like a cup of coffee and a freshen up?'

I stared into her face for a moment, trying to put myself back together. 'Yes please, I would love a cup of coffee, thank you and I do need a bit of a freshen up.'

I reached to open the shade on the window. It was still dark outside, but I left it open anyway. My coffee arrived in a mug and I thanked Michelle. I sipped the coffee. It was hot and refreshing and it hit the right spot.

I went to the washroom where my clothes had been laid out for me. I very much appreciated that. After I had freshened up, I went back to my comfortable armchair where a plate of bacon and eggs were waiting for me and another mug of coffee, along with a tall glass of icy cold water.

'Good morning gentlemen, did you sleep well?'

Frank replied he had, but stated there's no substitute for your own bed.

I said, 'Yes Frank. I learnt that a long time ago. A motel room can be the loneliest place in the world.'

After I finished my breakfast, I continued to look out of the window whilst sipping on my lovely, hot coffee and looking at the lights of ships and vessels anchored in the bay.

I could hear the noises of the aircraft preparing to land. Daylight was just coming over the horizon. I watched the ground coming up underneath us and I could see the runway. It was a very smooth landing, but I still felt myself moving forward in the seat as the aircraft was braking. I thought that was a short landing! The aircraft taxied to its refuelling spot; the pilots shut everything down, came out of the cockpit and disembarked.

Michelle put three drinks on the table. I looked at my two colleagues. 'It's always good to be on the ground, isn't it?'

They nodded an acknowledgement and took their seat belts off. I did likewise.

I sipped my coffee with my eyes closed, then put the mug back down and made myself comfortable.

CHAPTER 4

I felt the aircraft moving but there wasn't any sound! They must be towing the aircraft to a holding spot. I opened my eyes. I was feeling a bit groggy. Frank was standing by the aircraft door. I glanced out of the window. There was a van parked outside with maintenance written on the side.

I heard Frank saying good morning to two gentlemen coming on board. One was a lot younger than the other. The older man had a grey beard and was carrying a small bag; it could have been for his tools or his lunch. He slapped Frank on his shoulder. 'How are you, Frank? Haven't seen you for quite a while.'

They all shook hands. Bill and I stood up and the man with the beard looked at Bill. 'How are you, Bill? How are your wife and children?'

'They're doing well. Can't keep up with the children, though.' The gentleman put his hand on Bill's shoulder and shook his right hand with affection.

Then he turned to me. 'So, you must be Trevor. We met some years ago in Walter Wright's office. I thought he was going to bring you to Singapore, but you had a young family and a beautiful wife. My name is Ian.' He turned to the other two. 'Trevor worked for an old friend of mine.' He shook my hand. He had a firm hand grip, but not a power play handshake.

Ian looked towards the galley. His eyes lit up and he shouted out, 'Michelle, Michelle!' He said to me, 'Excuse me please Trevor.' He stepped forward and put his arms around Michelle and held her, then he held her at arm's length and with sadness said to her. 'I miss your granddad. He could be a bloody headache, but I do miss him.'

'Trevor, anybody seeing us would think we are a maintenance crew. You have to think a little differently in Singapore. Business and life move so much faster. It's good to have the company getting sorted out again, and to know who is running it.' He chuckled to himself. 'And these two vagabonds are the best you can have backing you. I would love to buy their contracts. Now Trevor, my mate Smithy and another mate bought a piece of land six years ago. We decided to build a hotel and apartments, but Smithy got sick and nothing was signed. We didn't know who owned the company, and it's taken five years to have his will ratified. A certain pigheaded bastard kept blocking it, but now you own it. Smithy always knew what he was doing. He was always one step ahead, always looking to the future. Concerning the land, he said we could buy him out. He agreed, and we shook hands. So where do we stand now, Trevor?'

'You made a deal with Peter Smith, and you shook hands so, to me a deal is a deal.' I put my hand out and shook his.

He grinned. 'It pays to be cautious, Trevor, and keep everything on the square.' Still looking at me, he handed the small briefcase to Bill.

As we sat down, I noticed a security van alongside the plane. I pointed out of the window. 'Are they a problem?'

Ian turned his head to look. 'Oh, this is my son Michael.' Ian nodded to him and Michael left the plane. I noticed him on the tarmac, talking to the security guards through the car window.

Ian said, 'We came through the back gate, thinking that we wouldn't be seen. Drugs here are the problem. This plane bypassed the normal taxiing procedures. We might have set ourselves up.'

Michael returned, 'As you said, Father, it's who you know that counts. Luckily, I went to school with those gentlemen.'

Bill had gone through the papers. 'Mr Evans, all the papers seem in order and I believe the price is right.'

A thought went racing through my mind: business is business.

'Now what would you think Peter would like? One apartment left to his granddaughter Michelle, and when she is not using it, it can be used for the hotel, so you pay all expenses, electricity and so on.' He looked at me. Michelle was grinning and Ian grinned at me.

'You're as shifty as he is, using his name first. How can I refuse?' He turned to me. Michael put his hand out and shook hers. 'You, young lady, are now the owner of an apartment. At the moment it is resting on a cloud, but I will put a building underneath it for you.'

Bill handed me the documents and a pen. I signed where he instructed me to, then handed the pen over to Michelle to co-sign her name next to mine.

I saw Bill studying this for a moment and he commented. 'Mr Evans, I was thinking of Michelle owning an apartment. Is that a conflict of interest? I think we need another signature. How about one of the pilots?'

Michelle brought some drinks, and we sat there talking about the good old days. Soon, both pilots returned. 'Gentlemen, I wonder whether you could come into the lounge and sign some papers for us as they are legal papers for land transactions.'

Both the pilots signed the paperwork and Bill handed the paperwork back to Ian, who added, 'Both Michael and me are Singaporeans so we can own land here, but originally we didn't have the money, so that is where Peter Smith came in. He lent us the money to purchase the land and we now want to pay that loan back. Thanks, Bill, we can now get to work. Michael and I will leave before anybody sniffs around. Catch up with you shortly.'

As Ian was going through the door, he gave me the sign of fidelity, nodded his head and was gone.

One of the pilots said to me, 'Our flight plan has been lodged, but we don't have permission to take off for another hour.'

'Then please sit down and have coffee with us.'

'Sir, we cannot do that, company regulations.'

'I have been a worker all my life. Sit down, I will look after the little people.'

I glanced at Michelle. 'Could you please bring these gentlemen coffee?'

Michelle said, 'Yes Sir.'

I looked at the two pilots. 'Do you work for me?'

'No Sir. We work for the company that services this aircraft. Our flight attendant, she works for the same company.'

My mind was racing ahead again. Does anybody know how she is connected to me, through Peter Smith? Has this somehow been arranged by Peter, very convenient? Start some small talk, Trevor.

'Have you ever spent time in Australia?'

'No, we haven't. We've just flown in, then out and haven't seen anything of the country.'

Small talk continued, but I learnt a bit about these two pilots. The way they worked impressed me. One of them looked at his watch and said, 'Time to warm her up, Sir.'

'Well, thank you gentlemen for our little chat. That didn't happen!' I winked at them.

One pilot said, 'It's always good to chat to Australians.' Then they went into their cockpit.

After about ten minutes, the jet started to move and come alive. Soon we were up in the air as quickly as before. We levelled out and the seat belt sign went out.

Michelle put a platter of food in front of me and another scotch and dry ginger. I looked at the platter of food. My mouth was watering.

Oysters, muscles, fish, prawns and scallops; there were also various slices of cheese and grapes. My two colleagues had the same. Somebody had been doing their homework. Who? The only name that came to my mind was Peter.

The next stop is Dubai. What's in store there? I finished my lovely meal and thoroughly enjoyed my scotch. I put my head back and dozed off to sleep.

CHAPTER 5

I don't know how long I slept; I awoke with a hand on my shoulder. I could hear Michelle's voice. 'We will land in two hours. I have put your clothes out in the washroom.'

'Thank you, Michelle.' I looked at my table, and there was a lovely mug of hot coffee there. I picked it up and started to drink and then I heard the snoring. Bill was stretched out on the comfortable armchair, his feet were up, his head was on the pillow and he was half covered up with a blanket. I thought he certainly could cut up firewood.

Frank was already up. He was standing in the galley with a mug of coffee. I noticed Michelle passing him, her hand brushing his, the way she looked into his face. I raised my eyebrows and thought, this could be interesting. I must watch this grow, it could be very useful in the future.

I changed into my clean clothes and came back to my seat. Bill was still snoring away. Michelle brought me my breakfast, along with another mug of coffee. The smell of bacon is very tantalising.

'Michelle, is there any way we can wake him up with a bit of amusement?'

She grinned and disappeared into the galley, and came back with a small towel. I could see it was warm, as steam was rising from it.

Bill's hand was resting on the arm of his chair. Michelle gently laid the towel upon it and went back to the galley. I have seen this little joke used before; it took a few minutes. Bill's eyes opened wide. He sat up and struggled to get off the armchair as his feet were in the up position, and he had his seat belt on; he flew to the toilet.

Frank stepped out of the galley, picked up the towel, and went back into the galley. I ate my breakfast, very much enjoying the show.

Bill came out of the toilet, and Frank asked him if he was okay. Bill, in a sharp voice, said he was.

Michelle commented, 'Waterworks are a little formal.'

Bill stared at them both, then grinned. 'He who laughs last laughs best. The game is a foot, Mr Watson.'

We were once again landing. I didn't realise how big Dubai was, only having been there once and that had been at night and we hadn't disembarked. Aircraft were everywhere. We had the same procedure as before. The jet engines were shut down, the pilots disembarked, and a fuel tanker pulled up alongside us and started to refuel the aircraft.

A white limousine pulled up alongside the aircraft. A chauffeur got out and opened the back door. Two gentlemen got out. One was dressed in a snazzy suit, the other in white robes with a headdress. Frank was waiting for them at the bottom of the stairs; they all came aboard.

I thought that in world events; I am just a bit of dust but here I am now, Mr Evans, playing games in a world where I don't belong. I was quite happy sitting on the bottom rung of the ladder, but now, I'm on the top rung of the ladder. Important people are coming to see me in my private aircraft!

I stood up as the man in white robes entered. The quality of the material in his robes made him look very impressive.

He bowed his head to me, whilst touching his forehead with his right hand. I stepped aside to greet him; he gave me a warm smile and said, 'We should greet each other like Australians,' and he put his right elbow out to me. I smiled and did likewise, our elbows touching. 'Please call me Ali.' He put his hand out and gestured to his colleague. 'This is Mr Dibley.' I nodded to him. He returned the nod.

I gestured to the armchairs for them to sit.

Michelle brought them ice-cold soft drinks in tall glasses and a plate of mixed fruit.

They picked up a glass. I did the same. We gestured to each other, took a mouthful, and returned the glass to the table.

Ali asked me whether we had a good flight.

I said, 'Yes, thank you. How can I help you, gentlemen?'

Ali said, 'It is a very complicated problem. First of all, my colleague,' he gestured to him, 'works for the government of Dubai. Speaking as you would better understand it in Britain, he would work for MI6. Our organisation went into a contract with Mr Smith to build a skyscraper next to his. It was agreed in the design of this skyscraper, that if circumstances should change in the economy, we could stop building and finish the top level and it would still be a very impressive building. Here is our problem. Your acting manager and his colleagues, who are in the upper circles of society, have decided to put a radio communications steeple on the very top, for themselves, not for society in general. We cannot get politically involved. It isn't in Dubai's interests. We do business with Russia, America, England, France and many other countries. This type of communication would be political suicide for us.'

I liked this man. He talks straight. 'So, you want me to stop it?'

'Yes, it would be in your interest as well.'

I sat there, studying him, trying to find the right answer for him. 'I understand perfectly what you're saying and the implications. I need time to think and work out a way to stop it and work out my political interests. If I own half of this skyscraper, I do not want anybody else taking advantage of it, for their gain.' I nodded to him. 'Please give me a little time.'

He picked up his glass, I picked up mine, and we gestured to each other, drained the contents of our glasses and put them back on the table.

Ali said, 'Next time you come to Dubai, I would appreciate it if you'd spend time with us. We could discuss many good things.' He bowed his head, touching it with his right hand. 'We will meet again.' The two men left the aircraft. I watched them get back into the limousine and disappear.

Michelle brought me a double scotch and dry. I put my hand out and took the glass, saying nothing. My mind was confused. How do I sort this problem out? Does Peter Smith already have the answers?

I slowly sipped my scotch. It felt good. Looking out of the window and seeing all the planes in the airport and the large city of Dubai made me feel very small and insignificant. I thought of Jackie and Charlie. I just wanted to pat him again and sit next to Jackie and hear her voice. Don't feed Charlie anymore. He is too heavy now, then she goes and gets me an ice cream, which she knows I will share with Charlie! I felt very lonely, yes; I miss them. I love them both so very much.

CHAPTER 6

'Trevor, Bill and I believe we should tell you something. We used to have drinks with a few colleagues after work. A young accountant who worked for the company spoke to us. He wanted to know what to do. He told us he had figures that didn't work out. We asked him what he meant. He said the company had two large factories, one of which made all types of leather work: belts, shoes, handbags, seat covers and leather items for the military. Another factory made many types of electrical equipment for buildings, lighting, electric motors for buildings and a large range of other items. Both companies were receiving more stores than they could use, but they hadn't increased production. Just as an example, I looked at toilet rolls. The number of people in the factory and the office, gauged by people working in the main building and they have twice as many as they need. Printing paper is the same, as are pencils and pens and even Stanley knife blades. The list goes on and on. What would you suggest we do?'

They looked at each other.

'What I would suggest is that you inform your superior, in writing, to protect yourself. Who is your superior?'

'Mrs Gilham.' They both replied. I didn't like the way they both looked at each other. 'If there's a problem, we always take it to the top.

That's the best advice we can offer. However, you'll need to find a way to shield yourself from the internal politics. He never joined us for drinks again; he simply vanished. That was three weeks ago.'

I sat there, reflecting on Mark Brunnel, the brilliant engineer. He was overseeing the construction of a steel vessel in a shipyard that had been contracted to build it sideways for a lateral launch. However, his calculations for the required materials didn't align with the inventory at the yard. To investigate, he observed the deliveries during the day and stayed behind at night after everyone had gone home. He waited and watched. Wagons turned up at 1 am. They loaded stores and equipment that had been delivered the previous day and then left the yard with them. Mark Brunnel followed them discreetly and watched them deliver his stores to another boat yard, which was owned by his contact. History sometimes has the answers to human behaviour, it always seems to take the same track, over and over. Self-centred arrogance. Can I use this to solve my problem?

'I thank both of you for sharing this with me. Your position as lawyers has its boundaries as to where you can go in company politics. By sharing this with me, I now know and can sort it out one way or another. Thank you. Now I must close my eyes and sleep, for when we get to England, it's all going to happen.'

I pushed the button to raise my feet and headrest, and I was asleep.

CHAPTER 7

Once again, I felt Michelle touch my shoulder. 'Trevor, it's time to wake up.' She had brought me a cup of coffee again. I went into the bathroom to prepare myself for England and on my return, my breakfast was waiting. Once I had finished, Michelle returned to pick up the dirty dishes. I asked her to sit down.

'Michelle, would you consider working for me directly, or should I say for your grandfather?'

She stared at me for a moment, then I saw the tears in her eyes. She reached forward, put her arms around my neck and said, 'Yes, yes, yes.'

I was a bit startled when she kissed me on the lips and said, 'I know granddad would want me to be part of sorting out his company.'

'Michelle, I want this to be between you and me. Nobody else is to know except our colleagues here. I want you to do some underground work for me.' I grinned at her and winked. 'Top secret stuff, my dear.'

She stared at me with a puzzled look. 'You say and do things the same as granddad. Are you sure you never met him?'

'Not that I can remember. I know I can find you any time I want through Frank.'

Michelle gave me a serious look, then frowned.

'Yes, I have been watching you. You have kept your feelings for Frank very discrete, but I'm an old man and I enjoy watching the game of youth. When the four of us are together in private, be natural. Now the question of stores. I have to know where they're going and to whom. I will let you know later what I want you to do.' I tapped my nose with my finger.

Michelle grinned, 'I'm in the Secret Service Department. Another cup of coffee Trevor?'

'Yes please, Michelle.'

I looked out of the window. Daylight was just touching the tops of small clouds, illuminating them in pink. I could see small aircraft below us, going this way and that, and then I could see the coast of England. I drank the last of my coffee. I had a feeling of anxiety and took a deep breath. Singapore put money in my pocket and the meeting in Dubai was a problem to solve. The stores, can I use this information to my advantage? As we were flying towards the airport, I watched the English fields, hedges and rows and rows of neat houses. The next minute we were touching down on the runway, it all happened again so quickly. The aircraft came to a stop. I was once again in England. I thought, *home again!*

Everything shut down and the two pilots came out of the cockpit and looked at me. I put my thumb in the air and said, 'Thank you.' They nodded and left. Michelle followed them and as she was leaving, she turned, smiled at me and winked.

Next thing I was going through customs with my two colleagues. There was a chauffeured car waiting outside the airport, and I was politely ushered into the back seat.

'Bill, could we go to Streatham Cemetery?' I asked. 'I would like to see my mother's grave.'

'Certainly Trevor.' He picked up a small receiver and spoke to the driver. I watched him punch the details into his GPS.

We turned into a small street and stopped at the cemetery gates. I got out and walked into the cemetery to my mother's grave. I looked down at the grave with tears in my eyes as I read, *Here lies Daisy May Evans.* 'Well Mum, I know that Dad is with you now and my brother Michael; he carried your photo in his wallet, but you probably know that. I'm tangled up in something I don't know about and I don't understand, but I do know the three of you will be standing alongside me and Michael will have the old tin bath. Love to all of you, I must go now.'

I took my handkerchief out of my pocket, wiped my eyes and blew my nose, then turned and went back to the vehicle. The driver had the door open for me. We were now heading for London. 'Bill, could the driver please drop me at the front entrance to the skyscraper?'

'Yes, Sir.'

I leant over to Frank. 'I hate the word *Sir.*' You would think we were in the Army, but I'll get used to it.'

The car stopped, and the chauffeur opened the door for me. I got out and stood looking at the glass entrance, and then I looked up and up at the glass-clad building. Many words went through my mind; to think I owned all of this! I looked to my right. There was a construction site, the base of the trumpet! The ground floor was well under construction. I couldn't see how big it was going to be because of the temporary walls around it, but on those walls were pictures of the interior. There were shopping centres, swimming pools, a casino, luxury apartments showing their décor, conference rooms and many other facilities. A sign said Sales Office, with an arrow and the address of Peter Smith's building. I stood there, trying to take it all in, but the noise of a helicopter above me made me look up just as it disappeared over the top of the glass building. I looked back to the glass foyer, turned around, and looked at the other side of the street. There was a coffee shop and a restaurant. I needed a little time to myself before going through that foyer. I crossed the road to the coffee shop and sat down at a table on the footpath, looking at the glass building and construction work.

A young lady asked me whether I would like tea or coffee.

'Coffee please, but I would prefer it in a mug, just a flat white, two sugars.'

The coffee turned up quickly, and I sat there sipping it, thinking. This construction site, this new skyscraper. How much money is it going to suck up to build? My money, Peter's money. Is there somebody using other people's money for their ends? When it's finished how much will it have cost me or my company? Where does it leave the company financially? I need people I can trust. Frank and Bill, Michelle, and Chris Ayres. Would she stay? I need people for me, not those who are influenced by others, especially when I'm not knowing what side of the fence they are on.

I saw Bill on the other side of the road, looking back and forward, looking anxious, then he saw me and walked over. 'Trevor, there are a few worried people.' He gave a small laugh. 'That don't have you under their control.'

'Well Bill, that puts things into perspective for me. I've never been really under control. I believe I have always been my own man.' I thought for a moment. 'Bill, would you like a cup of coffee?' I looked at him straight in the face. I'm now playing games.

He smiled, 'Yes Trevor, I would.' A waitress turned up and Bill asked for a white coffee, no sugar. Another waitress delivered his coffee.

'Hello Bill, how are you?' the waitress said.

'I'm doing very well, thank you. How are Cathy and the children?'

'Can't keep up with them, Bill.'

Trevor, can I introduce you to my wife's sister, Lesley?' I stood up and shook her hand. 'Lesley, would you care to sit with us for a moment?' She looked me straight in the face, trying to work me out.

Bill said to her, 'This gentleman has taken over Peter Smith's organisation.' She raised her eyebrows and sat down.

'How is business in general?' I asked her.

'Not good Trevor.'

'Why isn't it good?'

'Well, we were doing well, making money, good money. We have had an excellent reputation over the years, then Covid set in. We have been struggling for two years now and we have kept the business going by using my husband's money to pay the staff. They are top people and I don't want to lose them. They have been very faithful and have been with us for a long while. We just started to get back on our feet and out of debt.' I could see the emotion in her eyes. The tears were there, but she had the strength to hold them back. 'But they have now put the rent up and it's too much for me. We can't make any money, we are just surviving. I open at 8.30 am and have bacon and egg sandwiches waiting for people to purchase. I close at 7 pm. It's a long day. I'm trying to find a way out, to close the restaurant, but it will cost me money which I don't have and where will my girls go? I'm sorry to burden you with my problems. You must have a lot of your own. Would you please excuse me?' She got up and went back into the restaurant, wiping her eyes with a tissue.

Bill sighed and said. 'She is a fighter Trevor, she won't give up. If she loses this business, she loses her home as well. She's extremely faithful to the people she employs.'

I thought, now who's playing games?

Bill finished his coffee.

'Well Bill, let's go on.' We got up and crossed the road and went up into the foyer. There was a big model of the building next door, the Trumpet. I stood staring at it and its many levels, but there wasn't anything on top for communications.

Inside the foyer was a nice reception area, done out in coloured marble. There were three receptionists behind the desk. I walked over to it and one of the young ladies said, 'May I help you, Sir?'

'Yes, my name is Trevor Evans. I am currently the owner of this business. You are on the front line and I'm very impressed with the way I've just seen you handle those clients and the way you are representing this company. I will be coming down to have a chat with you all sometime in the future; just a friendly chat. Thank you, ladies.' I shook hands with each of them.

As I looked around the foyer, I noticed it had lots of modern art and some ridiculous paintings, which weren't my style at all. At the far end of the foyer, opposite the elevators, there was quite a large restaurant. The tables and chairs were not in very good condition and in my mind that brings down a restaurant quite a lot. Another two ladies were sitting at a desk with computers, next to the model of the Trumpet. They looked very smart and professional. I walked over to them. 'Bill, follow me,' I said. 'Good morning ladies, my name is Trevor Evans. You represent sales for the Trumpet.' They both smiled. 'That's a good name, isn't it? So, what do you offer your clients?'

'Well, you see the screen here, if they ask us questions we can bring it up on the screen, displaying what it will be like, with views of the theatres, shopping centres, swimming pools and the many other questions they will want to ask. We will then talk to them privately regarding costs and finances and when the various stages will become available.'

'Thank you, very professional.' I looked at them for a moment. I detected slight accents. 'Where do you both come from?'

'Dubai, Sir.'

'I hope to talk with you both later.' I nodded to them and started to walk towards the lifts. A young lady came towards me in an electric wheelchair, with an older lady walking behind her. She would have been in her 60s and the young lady in the wheelchair was crying. I couldn't help myself. 'Excuse me, why are you crying?'

The older lady with her looked very angry and she spoke sharply. 'My daughter has studied at university. She has four degrees in Business Management and Accounts. She has had six job interviews with various companies today and has been turned down by all of them.'

I looked at the wheelchair but still asked the young lady the question. 'Why have you been turned down?'

'They haven't exactly said, they've just played the tactful game.'

I studied the young lady, trying to put things together in my mind. She is young; she has her business degrees, she could work for me if she fights for her future. I put my hand out. 'Could I have your resume please?' I gave it to Bill. 'My name is Trevor Evans. This company is mine. You, young lady, will only answer to me, nobody else, now your name is?'

'Jodie Howard.'

'Very pleased to meet you, Miss Howard. Could you follow me, please?'

I walked back to reception and said to the three receptionists. 'This young lady is Jodie Howard. I want her to spend a week with you all, getting to know who is who and what is what. She will be working with us in the future. Could one of you take her down to the accessible toilets and see if she requires anything there to aid her? I will come back to you. Now, if you ladies will excuse me, I have games to play!' I nodded to Bill.

We entered the lift and Bill said to me, 'Are you sure you never met Peter Smith? You think and act exactly the same way he did.'

I shrugged my shoulders and thought, is he in my mind? I watched the numbers in the lift flashing past.

'We are going to the top,' Bill said. 'The top floors are for the hotel. Management uses the restaurant of the hotel.'

The lift doors opened and Bill walked out of the lift and stood slightly to one side. I stood for a moment, looking at the décor of the hotel. It was very impressive. They had blended the old with the new and there were beautiful shrubs and flowers in neat little boxes. Statues of animals and women. I liked the statues of women. They took the seriousness out of life. Bill led me into a room with windows that let you see the view of London. People were standing around a table that had been set for lunch. They all politely nodded to me. I nodded back.

One gentleman stepped forward, he was well dressed in a blue suit, waistcoat, white shirt and red tie and his initials were on the cuffs of his shirt. He had a very arrogant look on his face, which disturbed me.

He introduced himself. 'I am Neil Gilham, Trevor.' He put his hand out. I put my hand out to shake his. He took my hand, but as he did, he turned his hand over, so his hand was on top of mine. The power handshake. He slightly raised himself on his toes, looking down at me. I looked at my hand, then looked up at his face and thought, wrong move, Mr Gilham. I don't know why, but I stepped forward, so he was slightly off balance and kicked his left foot out from underneath him, making him fall backwards. I kept hold of his hand so that his head didn't hit the floor and then let his hand go. Everyone in the room looked shocked and then they smiled.

An extremely beautiful looking woman with blonde hair and tight-fitting clothes said in a very loud voice, 'What do you think you're doing?'

'I do not accept arrogance from my staff. I believe I have established a line of command. I am Australian, don't play games with me. I am a practical man and I don't like bullshit, so if I ask you a question, talk to me straight. So, you are Mrs Gilham, I presume, and I am Mr Evans to you both.'

Mr Gilham was getting back off the floor, tidying his hair and making sure his suit was in place.

'Now we are off to a good start. I want to get to know all of you but today but I won't remember your names as it's been a very long trip. However, I will remember your faces, so if we could enjoy our lunch together and just chat.'

Bill ushered me to a chair, and I sat down. Mr. Gilham sat down next to his wife and said nothing, whilst she just scowled at him. I thought to myself, typical schoolyard bully. He will get somebody else to do his dirty work for him. I asked in my mind, did I put him on the floor or was it Peter Smith? I enjoyed it though, but now I am the captain of this ship and the line of command has been established.

Everybody was looking at me. 'I am looking forward to working with you all and I know you're all wanting to ask the same question as to why Peter Smith has left me his company and all his assets. I don't know, I'm not an educated man. I'm self-taught in everything I've done. I've been in the heavy haulage and mobile crane industry for most of my life and have been quite successful. I could only go so far in my career because of my lack of education. I know that anybody who has a disability uses others to help them; we all have disabilities, so, if everybody in this organisation realises that and works as a team, helping each other, we will be successful in taking this organisation into the future.'

I could smell pea and ham soup and realised just how hungry I was. Waiters were putting bowls of soup in front of us. After soup, we had a typical English roast dinner, followed by fruit and ice cream for dessert. Everybody was talking to each other. They seemed quite relaxed. Mr And Mrs Gilham were very quiet. While we were drinking our coffee, various individuals asked me about Australia and our way of life. They wanted to know about kangaroos, koalas, wombats and Tasmanian devils. They also wanted to know about the Barrier Reef and its beauty.

I stood up. 'Ladies and gentlemen, thank you for having lunch with me. I've enjoyed your company. I intend to meet all of you individually and we will discuss your positions, ideas, and thoughts. Thank you. Mr. Farquhar, please show me to Mr. Smith's office. Mr and Mrs Gilham, please come and see me in half an hour in Mr Smith's office.' I turned and left with Mr Farquhar.

In the lift, I said to Bill. 'I've got to phone Jackie, but it has to be at the right time of the day in Australia. Could you please inform HR that I have employed Jodie Howard? Then I felt the first wave of jet lag come over me and I felt a small shiver come all over my body. I knew it was just nerves. The lift doors opened, and I stepped out and followed Bill.

I wondered what floor we were on but thought, I will pick it up soon enough. We went through glass doors into a small office. There were many computers on the desks, but nobody was sitting there. There was a large door, beautifully panelled. Bill opened it with a key and then handed the key to me. I held it in the palm of my hand and, looking at it, I felt that small shiver again. What's in store now? Is Peter Smith with me? This is his office. Should I let him call the shots? Bill pushed the door open, and I walked into a beautiful office. It had my type of furnishings, all of very good quality. There was an elegant green Chesterfield couch and armchairs. A coffee table in front was beautifully made, and the desk was in front of glass windows. Just how old was the desk? It had carved legs and was topped with a leather pad. There was a glass cabinet against the wall, upon which was a replica schooner, complete with sails. Further along the wall was a beautiful model of a steam yacht. I fell in love with it instantly. There were many paintings on the walls of people and seascapes. I looked at one of them and grinned to myself. It was a Neil Savage. I had one of those at home. There was another desk which I thought looked like a lady's desk.

Bill saw me looking at it. 'Yes, that was Chris's desk.' I walked over to the window and looked down at the new tower. From here I could see the full size of the project. It was like a city of its own.

Bill said, 'There is a bathroom and a day room at the far end.'

'Yes Bill, that is something I might need, a bathroom.' I went into the bathroom and washed my face with cold water, then looked at myself in the mirror. You poor old sod, what have you got yourself into? I shook my head and noticed that the mirror wasn't clean and there was dust on the bench. I walked into the day room. It had a beautiful brown leather couch with pillows at one end. It looked like it would be oh so comfortable to lie down on and have a nap. There was a beautiful old leather armchair with a table alongside it. There was a newspaper on the table and a glass. I picked up the newspaper and read the date. It was almost five and a half years old! I looked at the pictures on the wall of the sailing vessels and then I noticed a very impressive-looking wall safe. There was dust on top of it but it had finger marks on the dial. Somebody had been trying to open it, but who? I walked back into the office.

'Bill, would there be any Sellotape in one of those drawers?' He produced the Sellotape and a pair of scissors. 'Come with me.' We went back into the dining room. 'See that fingerprint here? Could you put some tape on top of it, peel it back slowly?' As he did so, he also noticed what I had seen.

'Interesting Trevor, isn't it? I have a friend in the Police Force, perhaps we could find out who they belong to.'

I smiled at him. 'Good thinking 99.'

We went back into the office and I sat down in Peter Smith's chair. Just then the door opened and in walked Mr and Mrs Gilham. They stood looking at me with that arrogant look, which so annoyed me. 'Don't you think it would have been polite to knock on the door before entering? Both of you sit down!'

Another man walked in behind them. Mr Gilham said, 'I would like to introduce you to my lawyer, Mr Ross Uren.'

This is becoming very interesting. What move on the chessboard is this? 'Good afternoon Mr Uren, please sit down. I would have ordered coffee but I don't have staff with me at the moment.' I gave Mr Gilham a sharp look.

Mr Uren said, 'I thought it would have been arranged.'

'Mr Uren, you do not work for me!'

He looked at Mr Gilham, who said, 'Mr Uren is a consulting lawyer.'

I wondered why we would need a consulting lawyer at this moment, so I informed him, 'I do not need a consulting lawyer, so why are you here?' I glanced towards Bill, then looked back at Mr Gilham. 'Why would you need your lawyer?' I grinned. 'You don't like my fun and games, Mr Gilham, Mr Uren?'

'No, no, sir, we have some documents for you to sign so the company can move on.' He took them out of his briefcase and placed them on the corner of the desk. Then he took a beautiful pen out from the inside of his jacket and handed it to me. He then picked up the first folder, but I reached out and took the whole bundle.

'At the moment I'm full of jet lag, so tomorrow my lawyer and I will go through the papers.'

'But Mr Evans, we need these papers signed today.'

I looked at him and thought pushy little fella, isn't he? 'Thank you, Mr Uren. I don't think we require you anymore today. My lawyer will show you out. Thank you. I'm quite sure Mr Gilham will ring you at his own expense when he needs you.'

Mr Uren didn't look at me, just got up and walked out with his empty briefcase.

'Now Mr Gilham, is there anything else you'd like to discuss?'

'Yes, there is. We need to get into the safe. There is paperwork in there. We need to sort out about any problems that we have had, to be able to move on.'

Mrs Gilham then said, 'We can arrange for a locksmith to open it.'

'Mrs Gilham, I have been here for one day and I have jet lag. As I said, I will sort out my problems with the safe in due course. It is my safe and if I should find there's paperwork you might require, you will receive it. Now, what I require is this office to be cleaned tonight and coffee, milk, sugar and biscuits provided. Do not clean the safe! Somebody has already tried to get into it. You wouldn't know who by any chance, Mrs Gilham, would you?'

Her expression didn't change, but her eyes fluttered back and forward.

'If you should know, I would be very interested. If there are any other questions you have for me, please ask. My door is always open to you. Now, I need to close my eyes and sleep, to be fresh for the morning. Thank you both.'

They got up, nodded to me and left, closing the door behind them. I put my hand up to Bill, not to say anything. I looked down at the papers in front of me. What is so important about this paperwork that it had to be signed right now?

I looked at Bill, and he smiled, shaking his head. 'I don't think anybody has talked to them like that for a very long time.'

'Bill, where do I sleep tonight?'

'You have a house at Maidenhead on the Thames. Mrs Smith lives there and your steam yacht is moored there. I took the liberty of informing her you would be there tonight. She's informed me that she will have Roast Pork for dinner for you.'

'Thank you, Bill. Do I use the helicopter or car?'

'Helicopter was your first choice. I will order it now.' He turned and left the office.

I looked again at the two mastered schooner model, got up and walked over to the cabinet. The schooner looked like it had been built for comfort. She had everything you could need. I wish that I had bought one long ago and I could have spent more time with my children, but work got in the way. Another regret.

I walked over to the model of the steam yacht. It was very classy, built for pure comfort, and it had beautiful lines and gentle curves. I looked at the brass plate in front of it. Built in Clyde, Scotland 1931 P, length 40 feet S, beam 12 feet, draft 4 feet; something was wrong, beam 12 feet, length 40 feet but who am I to argue with them? I went back to the desk and sat down. I was looking down at the folders and felt a wave of jet lag come over me and thought, I'm too weary and tired for this.

Just then, Bill walked in. 'All flights are arranged. Are you ready Trevor?'

'Yes, I am.' I picked up the folders and followed him. The next moment, I was in the air and the pilot was looking down at Bill, who waved us goodbye.

CHAPTER 8

I watched London slide away underneath us, and soon we were flying over the English countryside. We landed on a beautiful lawn surrounded by trees. There was a beautiful English cottage. It looked perfect, with honeysuckle draping over the doorway, flower boxes on the window ledges and the windows had tutor-style diamond lead-light windows. In the distance, I could also see a steam yacht tied up at a mooring.

The pilot got my suitcase out of the helicopter and showed me to the house. As I followed him, a lady stepped out of the house and said, 'Hello Trevor, we've been waiting for you, come in. My name is June.'

I followed her through the door. Wow, I felt mesmerized. This beautiful old English cottage had oak beams on the ceiling, and the stonework around the fireplace was beautiful. There were two high-back chairs facing the fireplace, and one had a table alongside it. Another smaller table had knitting on it. The other bigger table had an ashtray with a half-smoked cigar and cigar box on it.

'I haven't had the heart to throw it away. I hated the bloody things when he was alive; they stink, but now he's gone, I miss the smell and him.'

June picked up a bottle of Scotch. 'Now take this Scotch down to Michael on the steam yacht. Her name is Lillie, and we call Michael,

Grumpy. You don't have to be polite to him; just tell him dinner will be ready in an hour and a half.'

I didn't ask questions, just turned and walked down to the moorings, passing the pilot who was standing by the helicopter. 'What time in the morning, Mr. Evans?'

'Let's make it 8.30 am.' I winked at him. 'I'm still on pm time.' I stopped walking and looked at the beautiful steam yacht. It was so well kept, with nothing out of place.

I heard an angry voice shout, 'What the hell do you want?'

I ignored him, took off my shoes and stepped aboard. He was a tall, thin man with a grey beard, wearing a T-shirt and trousers. He had bare feet and piercing eyes. I put the bottle of scotch on the table. 'Get two glasses, Grumpy.' I sat down.

He put his hands on his hips. 'Who the hell are you?'

'My name is Trevor Evans.'

For a moment he just stared at me. Then he said, 'You took your time getting here, didn't you?'

He turned around, picked up two glasses and put them on the table. I opened the bottle of scotch and poured. He picked up his glass and swallowed it straight down. I sipped mine, thinking of my jet lag.

Michael said, 'I needed that. The blasted Smithy left me all alone. We've been mates all our lives. We restored this vessel together, and that idiot Gilham and his wife, Barbie Doll, who doesn't like water, want to sell it. So, you seem to know my name. When Smithy realised he was sick and was going to die, he knew the company was going to have problems. His granddaughter Michelle was not ready to take over the responsibility. She needs more life training and needs to be more streetwise. He had a good friend and business partner in old Wally. Wally gave Smithy your name and told him all about you and I put a plan together.'

I poured some more scotch into his glass; he swallowed it straight down again. I could see his eyes starting to well up with tears. He turned and went to the stern of the yacht. I left him alone.

I noticed a brass plaque on the bulkhead: Lillie – built on the Clyde, Scotland, 1934, 80 ft in length and 12 ft beam, steam-propelled. Grumpy's voice behind me said, 'She was built with the best; she was pure quality.'

'Grumpy, would you have a pencil and paper, please?'

'Yes.'

I wrote the figures on the brass plaque. 'Now tell me, Grumpy, what do you know about the Gilhams?'

'Well, Smithy had a mate. They went to the war together, and when they came back, his mate became a big banker. He was a top money person, and his wife thoroughly spoilt their son, who was a schoolyard bully. He might have put a little bit of pressure on Smithy to employ him. He started at the bottom and worked his way up the ladder. He was doing quite well, although still very arrogant, but you aren't going to take that out of him. Then he married Naomi. Where she came from, nobody knows. After Smithy died, she became a real bitch. She is very intelligent, and she is very good at manipulating people. She's also very sly and untrustworthy. Nobody can do anything because the Gilhams are at the top of the system.'

'I can tell you this, Grumpy, nobody is selling this vessel. I think we had better go up for dinner now.' I swallowed the rest of my Scotch.

As we walked up the lawn, Grumpy said to me, 'There are ten acres here. The Gilhams want to sell half of it, with the river frontage split into 2-1/2 acre lots. I get confused as to who owns this. I believe you do, so could you keep reminding me, please?'

We got back to the cottage where dinner was waiting for us, and we sat down at a beautiful table. I kept looking at the embroidery on the tablecloth. My wife, Jackie, would have appreciated this, as well as the flowers in the silver vase in the centre of the table. Frank walked in from the lounge, followed by Michelle and another lady. I winked at Frank and Michelle. 'You two don't waste any time!'

Frank replied, 'Allow me to introduce Chris Ayres.'

I stood up, a little surprised, and put my hand out to shake hers. 'I have wanted to meet you; please call me Trevor.' We shook hands, and everybody sat down at the dinner table.

Michelle asked Frank to open the wine. He didn't argue but said, 'Trevor drinks scotch and dry ginger.' She disappeared for a moment and returned with my scotch and dry.

I looked at Chris, who said to me in a very businesslike voice, 'I would be delighted to work alongside you. The only thing I would require is a company car, a RAV4 Toyota. Mr Smith discussed you with me and the procedure about what was going to happen; it just took a little longer than he thought.'

I raised my eyebrows. 'Well, that takes care of that problem Chris. Have you been dismissed from the company?'

'Yes, I have been completely paid out.'

'Then would it be convenient for you to be my secretary and to start at 9 am tomorrow? Frank, could I leave it in your hands to sort out the paperwork?'

Chris looked at me seriously. 'Could I have the pleasure of handing Mrs Gilham the paperwork? Before Peter died, she hadn't been a problem, but now she thinks she owns the company.' She looked straight at Grumpy, who was smiling. 'And you shut up; things have been sorted out for you.'

Michelle reached down as she put my glass on the table and said quietly, 'He has asked her to marry him. We all stay out of it, too hot!'

Change the subject, Trevor. 'I've got to phone Jackie at home before I go to sleep, so don't let me forget Mrs Smith.' I looked at Chris.

'Yes, I think that's important, but before you put your weary head down, there is something we must show you after dinner.'

I thoroughly enjoyed the roast pork and apple sauce, the apple crumble and the ice cream, which was followed by coffee. I was very content, I'd had a good meal, solved some problems and was ready for sleep after I phoned Jackie back in Australia.

Chris said, 'Follow us, Trevor.'

We went through a hallway to a large bookcase full of books. June ran her hand up to the top of the bookcase, and it slid sideways, exposing a door to a passage. Chris opened the door, and I walked into the room. I didn't know what I was seeing. It was a beautifully furnished room with five desks, upon which were computers. Chris said, 'These computers are linked with the computers in the company building, so that Peter knew exactly what was going on throughout his organisation.'

'So, all the records are still here?' I asked her.

'Yes, Trevor. He thought of everything; he was hard to keep up with.'

'I'm afraid you'll have to excuse me. I need to sleep. I'll go through this in the morning.'

Michelle showed me to my room and handed me her mobile phone so that I could phone Jackie.

The phone answered, and I said, 'Hello, Trevor here, Jackie. I'm having trouble with jet lag at the moment. It's been a full-on day here. Is everything all right at home?'

'Yes, Trevor, Stephanie is bringing the children down tomorrow, and we are all going out to lunch.' Jackie chuckled. 'We're having honeyed prawns.' We chatted a bit longer, and I said that I would phone her tomorrow.

CHAPTER 9

The next thing I knew, I opened my eyes and noticed it was still dark. I didn't even remember going to bed! I sat on the edge of the bed and turned on the small light. My watch said 5 am. I got up and went to the bathroom. Was yesterday just a dream? Looking around the room, I realised the answer was no! There was a suit on a suit chair along with a clean shirt, underwear and socks. I picked up the underwear and went into the bathroom to have a shower. The hot water on my head and back straightened me up, and I so enjoyed it. I looked into the mirror and thought I must shave. I got dressed, put my shoes on and thought, well I'm ready for the day, whatever may come forth, coffee old chap!

I walked to the kitchen. June was sitting down at the kitchen table, sipping her cup of tea. 'You're up early, June,' I said.

'Good morning, Trevor. Peter was always up this early. It was the only time we could talk.'

'June, Grumpy told me Peter had a friend called Wally Simpson. I know a Wally Simpson back in Australia. He was one of the directors of the company I worked for. He had a clothing store.'

June smiled at me. 'Yes, Trevor, the same Wally; it's a small world, isn't it?'

'Yes, it is. Wally started working at our Myer store. That's where he learned his trade, and then he began working for himself. He was very successful.'

'Breakfast Trevor? Bacon and eggs, and I believe you like onions as well.'

'Yes, I do.'

June put a big mug of coffee in front of me and a small bowl containing my medication. 'I used to put Peter's tablets out for him as well. If I didn't remind him, he would forget.'

Grumpy walked into the kitchen and in an appropriate voice said, 'I couldn't sleep. One day I'm gonna get a shotgun to those blackbirds.'

June said to him sharply, 'You leave my blackbirds alone. When they sing, they make me happy.'

Chris walked in through the back door, wearing her dressing gown, and then Michelle walked in also wearing her dressing gown. I said, 'Good Morning Michelle.'

She smiled at me. 'G'day mate, how are you going?'

I winked at her. 'Actually, very well. Could you phone your lover, Frank, and ask him to come straight here? We are now going to play games. Ask him not to tell anybody where he is going.'

June said, 'Don't talk to him too long Michelle, your breakfast is ready.'

My breakfast turned up, and my coffee cup disappeared. I looked at my bacon and eggs, then looked at the floor alongside me and felt a twinge of loneliness. I normally give our dog Charlie bits of my bacon. It's like a ritual. I miss you, Charlie.

The bacon was thick, not the normal stuff they have in England, and I enjoyed it very much. My coffee mug turned up again with hot coffee. I thanked June and studied the others at the table. I'd never had a business secretary before. Chris was quick; she always seemed to be one step ahead. Sharpen up Trevor, that's why she's a good secretary. Grumpy is a good friend you can talk to and bounce ideas off of, and you'll get a straight answer back, no politics. Michelle, did Peter want her to take over his company? I believe it is rightfully hers. Is that really what my job is? To train her to take over the helm? I like June; she is the perfect wife for a businessman. She had everything prepared for him; she knew when to be the perfect partner, especially when he was tired and weary. Make sure she's fully protected, Trevor!

Just then, there was a knock at the back door. Frank walked in and went straight up to Michelle, whilst saying good morning to everybody.

June said, 'Sit down, Frank.' She had breakfast ready for him, and he sat down next to Michelle.

I waited until he'd finished his meal, then I said, 'I want you to come straight here every morning. Don't tell anybody you're here. You and Michelle will sit down in front of those computers and go through everything. Find out where the money is going, if there is any skulduggery going on and then put it all on a file so that I can read it. Keep it simple; I'm just a simple man. Michelle, get to know your granddad's company. Get into his mind, and if you have any problems, please ring. Chris, talk to her when she gets home. Frank, you are a lawyer; put your skills to work. I want everything tidied up, with ethics and standards. I believe you're not just working for me; you're working for Peter Smith. Michelle and June, make it a game and enjoy it. Chris, do you want to come with me in the helicopter?'

'No, thank you, I don't like boats or helicopters.'

Frank smiled at me. 'I expected that Chris,' he said, 'your car will be here at 8.30 am.'

'Thank you, Frank.'

'Any time, Chris.'

'Frank, could you talk to me about a young accountant I met on the plane? If you could look into that and put some documents in a file concerning it, I would appreciate it,' I said.

'Yes, I will do that, and it will be fun.'

'Michelle, if you were the captain of a sailing vessel in a storm and you gave a command, would you expect it to be done?'

She frowned at me. 'Yes, I would.'

'And, if you were having dinner with your lover, you wouldn't give him a command, would you?'

'No.'

'Well, in the computer room, you are in command at all times, do you understand what I'm saying?'

'Yes, I do.'

I smiled at Frank. 'You're a healthy man, keep your hands to yourself in the computer room.'

He bowed and put his hand up to his forehead. 'Yes, Boss.'

I smiled and then heard the helicopter landing. 'Excuse me.'

I went down to my room, picked up a folder, took out the relevant piece of paper and put it into the inside pocket of my jacket. I went back to the kitchen, then June and Grumpy walked out with me. June put her arms around my neck and kissed me on the forehead. She smiled at me.

'You are a spoilsport. Two young lovers together, you certainly know what will happen.'

Grumpy said, 'I think you already know what Smithy wants.'

'Just keep talking to me Grumpy, you're the best advisor I've got.'

I climbed into the helicopter, and we were on our way. I looked down and saw the little cottage and Grumpy walking with June.

CHAPTER 10

Landing in a helicopter on the top of a building was not my cup of tea, but I took a couple of deep breaths and put up with it.

Once we had landed, I went straight to my office. When I walked in, a lady was cleaning the windowsills; she turned around rather sharply.

'Oh, excuse me, Sir, I should have been finished by now, but the office hasn't been cleaned for such a long while. My name is Margaret, and I have been cleaning Mr. Smith's office for a very long time. I wanted to do it right for you. I am leaving this week as they have ended my employment and are putting on contractors.'

'So, Margaret, you were Mr Smith's assistant?'

'Yes, I was, and I did all the small things he wanted.'

'Do you want to leave?'

'No, I don't. I have only my husband to look after, my daughter and my two grandchildren. I really need the income.'

'Chris Ayres will be in shortly; she will sort out things for you.'

'But she's left the company.'

'This is her rightful place, as it is yours. You take as long as you like to clean. Could you please get two coffees, one for me and one for yourself?'

She put her hands together and started to cry. 'I didn't know what I was going to do; this has always been my home. Mr. Smith called me fussy, and we gave each other cheek. I enjoyed working for him so much, and I lost my best friend when he died. I will get your coffee.'

I could hear her crying in the kitchen.

I took the piece of paper out of my pocket and looked at the numbers. I also looked at the numbers on the model of the steam yacht. 1934 P 40 S. Trevor, you are simple! He's giving you the combination to the safe. Left 1934, right 40. I walked up to the safe with the numbers and I thought, no, don't open it. I went back to my desk and opened the first file in my bundle. The first piece of paper was all about my permission to put a company on the Stock Exchange; shares would be purchased in the company to make it a public company. The first words that came into my mind. 'Shifty, bloody sly ******.'

I opened one of the drawers on the desk, looking for a red pen, and found it. I put a red line through where I was supposed to sign and put the papers back into the folder and put it to one side. A hand put a mug of coffee down on the desk next to me, and she said, 'This was Mr. Smith's mug.'

'Thank you, Margaret, did you get one for yourself?'

'Yes, I did.'

'Could you bring it in here and drink it with me?' She looked at me; she appeared a little worried.

'Is that the right thing to do, Sir?'

'I'm Australian, and in this office, I remain an Australian, so please sit down and talk to me.'

She disappeared and came back with her coffee.

'I assume your husband isn't working?'

'No, he's now eighty-four. I'm 10 years younger than he is. He takes care of the grandchildren. Our daughter lost her husband; she works in the coffee shop across the road.'

Just then the door opened and in walked Chris. When the two women saw each other, they called out each other's names and embraced each other like long-lost friends. I picked up my coffee and slipped out. I wouldn't have been able to get a word in edge-wise, anyway. They kept on talking without a break, then they went into the kitchen. I thought I should leave them alone and kept drinking my coffee. After a while, they came out, wiping their eyes.

Chris walked over to her desk and put her bag down. She put both her hands flat on her desk and then patted it as if it were alive. She turned around and looked at me. She was still crying.

'Trevor, I miss him so much. I never thought I'd be back in this room, at my desk.'

'Chris, when you've composed yourself, could you phone our lawyer Bill, and ask him to come and see us, please.'

'You'd better be prepared; I could start crying again.'

If this crying goes on, I will start crying as well. 'Margaret, you haven't finished your coffee. Now, you were saying your daughter works across the road.'

'Yes, now that they have put the rent up, it's hard to make ends meet financially.'

We could hear Chris on the phone 'Hello Janet, yes, it's Chris here.' There was a short pause. 'Yes, I'm back. I'll talk to you later. Could you please ask Bill to come up to the office, and if he argues with you, tell him I still have a house brick in my bag.'

I could hear them both laughing; it must be an old joke. Then she said, 'Yes, Peter's picked the right man. See you later.'

There was a loud knock on the door, and Bill walked in. He looked straight at me. 'Good morning, Sir.' Then he looked at Chris. 'Good God! I've got troubles now.' He walked over to Chris, who threw her arms around his neck.

'Bill, if you give me any trouble in the future, I will enjoy it because I've missed you and your sense of humour.' She continued cuddling him. 'How are Kathy and the children?'

'They are doing well, Chris. When I tell Kathy you're back, she's going to be so happy.'

'Bill, Chris, follow me.' I walked up to the safe and put in the combination: left 1934, right forty. I pushed the little handle down, and the safe opened! I smiled.

Chris said, 'Peter knew you would find the combination.'

'Did you know the combination?'

'Yes, I did.' She had a big smile on her face. I took out four big envelopes, one of which was addressed to Michael. That envelope was quite thick. The next envelope was addressed to Joe Clark, Devon Boat Yard. It was also thick. The next two envelopes were addressed to me.

I opened the first one and took out the paperwork. I read the first page.

Trevor, I apologise for putting this burden on you, but there are very few men who can put things together for Michelle. She needs your natural talents to prepare her to take over my organisation. You are very streetwise, compassionate and understanding, and you know when to put your foot down and bring people down to size. You don't like yourself when you do it because you hurt people, but sometimes it's needed to run an organisation such as this. Look after my little Tootsie. I know you will look after my beautiful partner. We have been married a long time, and she's always stood by me, no matter what. When I came home tired and weary, she understood and gave me the compassion I desperately needed. Some people have a goldmine; I had my beautiful June. I love her so dearly; she's my little Chestnut.

He had underlined Tootsie and Chestnut in red.

Put your full faith in Chris; she's been with me from the beginning. She has been our best friend always. If you need another man to talk to, to bounce the ball with, Grumpy's your man. He will give you a few different directions to think about. He's always had his hand on my shoulder to guide me and I can't express my feelings for him, they go too deep, the grumpy old sod! Bill and Frank, my Lawyers are always watching my back, no task is too hard for them, they are my Oak Trees. I can lean on them anytime, look after them, and if they ask you for a small favour, just do it. My accountant is my good friend, Neville. He's as straight as a die; his manners and integrity cannot be questioned. It has to be right or not at all. Neil Gilham can do good work and make money, but instead of putting his foot down, he seems to bully people, which naturally doesn't go down too well with clients, especially when they owe you money. Naomi Gilham is good at marketing and sales, but you have to keep your foot on her as she is a control freak and very streetwise. I've left you with the best team; they are my team. Could you deliver Grumpy's envelope and Joe's ASAP, take Bill and Michelle with you, I will always be standing behind you.

It was signed, Peter Smith.

'Chris, could you order a helicopter, please? There will be four of us.'

Chris picked up the phone and pressed a button. 'Hello Jarrett, yes, I'm back. Trevor Evans would like a helicopter for four passengers, yes, right now, please. Mrs Gilham will have to find her transport for her golf day!' Chris gave a chuckle. 'You enjoy it, Jarrett, and I won't repeat what you've just said. Thank you.'

Bill took an envelope out of his inside pocket. 'This envelope is for Margaret.' He handed it to me. I looked at him, and he winked as I handed the envelope to Margaret. She looked a little surprised but took the envelope. She opened it, took out the paperwork, with a confused look on her face.

'Look at it, Bill,' she said.

'Yes, Margaret, it is a four-bedroom ground-floor flat. It is all yours; you own it. The insurance has been paid for five years, so it is being painted out now. There is a letter inside for you.' She slumped down in a chair, just staring at the envelope.

Chris walked up behind her and put her arms around her shoulders. She looked at me with tears in her eyes again. 'If you gentlemen could leave us together, we are having a difficult day, albeit a good one.'

CHAPTER 11

I picked up the folders off my desk and the two large envelopes. The next moment we were again in the helicopter heading for the house. We arrived in no time at all and landed on the lawn. We got out, and I went into the house. June was in the kitchen preparing lunch.

'How's your day going, June?'

'Not good, they can't find the passwords to the computers, Trevor.' She looked at Bill. 'How are you, Bill?'

'Doing well but a bit confused.'

'That makes two of us. Trevor, Bill, follow me.' We followed her into the computer room. Frank and Michelle were sitting in front of the computers and turned around quickly when we entered.

Michelle said, 'This is very frustrating; we can't find the passwords.' Then she looked at Bill, who was looking at the computers.

'What is all this?'

'These are Peter's computers. They are tapped into the company.'

Bill said, 'Shifty old fox!'

Michelle said, 'I wouldn't have a clue to the passwords.'

I put my hands on her shoulders. 'Try putting in Tootsie.'

She turned around. 'How do you know that is what he used to call me?'

'Put it into the computer,' I said.

Michelle did, and the computer came to life.

She yelled out, 'I'm in, I'm in!'

'Frank, try Chestnut on your computer.'

He did so and his computer also came alive.

Michelle said, 'How did you know that?'

June replied with a smile. 'When Peter and I first met, I was fourteen and a half. We used to pick up chestnuts for a farmer to get extra money to spend on food. His nickname for me was always Chestnut.'

'June, Peter has left us all the information we require. Come with us now; we have another minor task to do. Michelle, could we all go down and see Grumpy? I'm sure he will need another bottle of Scotch!'

Frank and Michelle turned off the computers and followed me. When we arrived at the steam yard, Grumpy was standing with his hands on his hips, looking confused but saying nothing. We all went aboard. I asked Michelle to give him the envelope. She reached out, took it and gave it to Grumpy, who looked at it very suspiciously.

'What is it?'

'I have a fair idea, but I don't know for sure.'

We all stood there waiting for him to open it. June said, 'Do you want me to open it for you?'

Grumpy said 'Yes' and handed it to her. June opened the envelope and looked inside. She took out a small envelope, folded the bigger envelope up, then opened the small one and took out the documents and read them. She looked up to Grumpy; you could see the emotion in her body as the tears started to flow.

'He has left you this vessel. It is now yours. Nobody can take it from you.'

Grumpy stared at her and said, 'They told me they were going to sell it.'

June said, 'It wasn't theirs to sell; the vessel belongs to you and Peter, and he has left his half to you. You now own it.'

Grumpy turned and went to the wheel. He was holding two spokes in his hands and was sobbing to himself, saying, 'She is mine. No, Peter, I know you're here. She is still ours, the river is ours, and we will be together until the end.'

June put her arms around his neck. 'When you have composed yourself, lunch is ready.' She climbed back onto the jetty and ambled back to the house. We knew she was crying and trying to compose herself. We all followed her slowly.

Peter had tied up another loose end.

When we got back to the house, I said to June, 'The day is running out fast, and we have to go down to a boat yard in Brixham, Devon. Michelle, you have another envelope to deliver. Let's go. June, I think you should come too.'

'Oh, what about my hair and clothes? I've got to change.' Before anybody could argue, she had gone.

Michelle quickly made some sandwiches, and as she was doing so, Grumpy walked in and looked at me seriously. 'Peter picked me up off the streets and gave me a family home. Now he's given me a steam yacht and enough cash to look after her.' He put his hand out and shook my hand. 'Thank you, Trevor. Anytime you want to go up the river, we are yours. Thank you.'

'Michael, we come from the same place, you and me. I too had a good friend who looked after me through the years.'

I walked back out of the house, onto the lawn and got back into the helicopter. Bill followed me and joined me in the back seat. I handed him the folders. 'Have a look through these, Bill.'

June climbed in the front, looking very pleased with herself. She smiled at me. 'I'm going to enjoy this. I know what we're going to do.'

Michelle climbed in alongside Bill and gave me a bundle of sandwiches. I nodded to the pilot, and we were on our way.

I opened the sandwiches and offered one to Bill and Michelle. I handed one to June, and she gave one to the pilot.

Bill started laughing. 'Trevor, you've taken care of that with the red pen.' He had opened the folder I had looked at earlier. As he opened the next folder, he nudged me and said, 'We've taken care of this one too.' He picked up the third folder and opened it. He said, 'That isn't going to happen either; it doesn't belong to them.' He looked at me. 'One is for the public company, the other is for the steam yacht, the other for the boat yard, the third one is for the subdivision of land. Now what's the fourth?' He raised his voice. 'This is stupid; it is for £1,000.000.00 of shares in the tower next to them. Mr Gilham thought you were going to be a pushover and just sign without reading them. The steam yacht and boat yard have been taken care of before Mr Smith died, so there wouldn't be any probate on them once we've delivered the documents to the boat yard. Mr Smith has cleaned up everything nicely.'

June started clapping her hands. 'I'm so much enjoying this. Don't play games with Mr Smith Mr Uren, he can still eat you alive.'

Bill said, 'I'm going to have to look into Mr Uren a little deeper. He is very good in the way he's put these documents together.' With a mouthful of sandwich, he said, 'These are damn good sandwiches. Are there any left?' June handed him another one, but he took two. I took one, Michelle took one, and the pilot had another one, so there was just one left for June.

I enjoyed watching the countryside and the small fields with hedges going around them; the woods sliding past us. I felt that feeling again, damn jet lag.

Soon we landed on a floating pontoon in Brixham harbour, and we all walked down the jetty to the boat yard following June and Michelle. I picked up the pace a bit and frowned at Bill. 'They have forgotten I'm an old man!'

'Trevor, they are on a mission, and when women are on a mission I have learned not to get in their way.'

Bill went to open the door to the office before the women got there, but they nearly knocked him over. The receptionist looked at June. You could see that she was surprised. 'Hello Mrs. Smith.' She noticed Bill and Michelle and looked straight at me.

'Oh, I'm Trevor from Australia.' I put my hand out and shook hers.

June said, 'Is Joe about?'

'Yes, he's in the yard. Oh, excuse me, this is Lisa, Joe's daughter.'

June said, 'Sorry, excuse me, I'm excited and forgot my manners.'

Lisa picked up a small microphone and spoke into it. 'Joe, could you please come to the office? It is important.' Then she turned to Michelle, saying, 'We haven't seen you for a very long time.'

'Lisa, I have been so busy studying business and trying to get my pilot licence. I've got three certificates done and have only one more to go. Trevor here is also keeping me very busy.'

Just then the office door opened and in walked Joe Clark. Seeing June, his eyes lit up. He put his arms out and embraced her. She cuddled him back, then gently shook him. 'Joe Clark, we had an understanding, you would ring me.' He looked at her seriously, then picked up a document from his desk and handed it to her. She read it.

'Joe, the dockyard is not for sale.'

She handed me the document, then said to Michelle. 'Please give Joe the envelope.' Michelle did, and he took it. He stood looking at it. He knew the writing on the envelope; he looked at me.

'You are Trevor Evans from Australia?'

'Yes, I am.'

'So, Peter's plan has been set in motion.'

He opened the envelope and took out a smaller envelope, opened it, took out the contents and read them. He then handed them to his daughter, and she read them. In an emotional voice, she said, 'The boat yard and harbour are not for sale; we own it! Dad, I've got to phone Mum.' Lisa went to the reception desk, took a tissue from the tissue box, then picked up the receiver and said, 'Mum it's happened, it's true, we own the boat yard. Michelle and June are here, and they have the title. Trevor Evans and the Lawyer Bill are here as well. Stop crying Mum, and get down here.'

Lisa came back into the office, wiping her eyes with a tissue. While we were waiting for Lisa, I had said to Bill, 'Could you put this piece of paper with the files where they will be safe, they will be the evidence we will need for Mr Uren.' I was gritting my teeth.

Joe chuckled. 'Peter talked about you; I think he's picked the right man. Michelle, the two mastered schooner is yours. What do you want me to do with it? At the moment it's in storage on dry land, but it needs to be back in water to keep its timbers swollen, to stop them from splitting.

Michelle replied, 'You have a boat charter business. If you could put her back in the water and use her for your business, that would be fine. She will be there for me when I need her, and that will pay for her mooring and upkeep.'

'Michelle, we will clean her up and anti-fowl her hull and give her a bit of paint and varnish, she will be like new. Trevor, can I use Bill to sort out a few other legal problems?'

I gestured to Bill, and he said, 'Certainly, but I would have to bring Kathy and the children with me.'

Joe grinned. 'You drive a hard bargain.'

I said, 'That means I will lose a helicopter for a day. Bill. Could you make it on a weekend? You wouldn't want the children to miss out on school.'

Michelle spoke very loudly. 'That means I can fly the helicopter and spend the day with Lisa.'

I shook my head. 'I've been outsmarted here, that is one of the three certificates you've got.' She gave a little seductive wiggle and a cheeky smile. 'Yes.'

'Well, that's Peter's little problem solved and everything's in place. I would love a Scotch and dry ginger.'

Joe said, 'I can fix that.' He went to the bar fridge, took out the dry ginger, took the scotch off the shelf, grabbed a bottle of wine and two glasses. Just then, there was a screech of tyres and Joe said, 'That's my wife.'

The office door opened, then his door burst open, and a rather large lady was standing in the doorway. She yelled out, 'June, you said Peter would take care of it, and he has.' They embraced each other, and without looking around, she said. 'Get the wine, Joe, and you, Bill, keep the cheek to yourself.'

Bill started laughing and said, 'You definitely will get a new set of tyres for your anniversary.'

She spun around and looked at him. 'My God, you're right, it's our anniversary today. Bill, you have a memory like an elephant.'

Joe said to me, 'I would have thought he might have told me first; now I'm in trouble. Trevor, this is my wife Harriet.'

Harriet said to Joe, 'Pour the wine.'

'Yes, dear.'

Lisa picked up the mic and said, 'Everybody come into the office, we have a celebration.'

The next moment the office was full of people with glasses in their hands, and wine going everywhere. Everyone was chatting, and cheering at the good news. It was just on dusk when we boarded the helicopter and took off waving to the people on the jetty. The pink glow over the sea and the setting sun was a beautiful sight to see. The lights on the foreshore were starting to twinkle.

We arrived back at the house, and I got out of the helicopter. We were tired; it had been a long day, but another really good day.

CHAPTER 12

June said. 'I'm not used to that type of cheek from you, Grumpy!' and she shook her spatula at him. 'But don't stop, I like it!' She put his coffee down in front of him, and he sat down, patting me on the shoulder.

Chris walked in the door. 'Good morning, all.' She sat down at the table. 'What is first on the agenda this morning, Trevor?'

'Chris, I would say the first part is over. We have sorted out the personal things for Peter; now it's the company's problem. I've got some reading to do first, then I'll spend some time with Neil Gilham; he must be getting itchy feet by now.'

Michelle walked in. 'I've got itchy fingers. I want to get back to the computers. We are having fun. Your young accountant is the manager of your hotel in Eastbourne.'

Chris's voice boomed out. 'Oh no. Barbara would be the best manager you could have. She made that business click, and it made money. I know she didn't get along with Mrs Gilham, but she made the clients happy and made money to boot.'

I heard the helicopter land, so put my bacon on my toast, picked it up, excused myself, and walked out to the waiting helicopter.

'Good morning, Jeffrey. We are going to my hotel in Eastbourne. Be as quick as you can.' I know I felt angry. I put up my hand to Jeffrey.

'No, Jeffrey, we had better take Michelle and Frank.' I could see Frank pulling up in his car. As he got out, I shouted to him. 'Could you get Michelle, please, and join us in the helicopter.'

They both got in the back. 'Take it away, Jeffrey,' and we were up in the air.

'Frank, Michelle tells me our young accountant is in Eastbourne.'

Michelle replied, 'And I don't think Barbara will be too happy Frank, she made him the Manager.'

'Whoops!' commented Frank.

I said to Michelle, 'As a woman, Michelle, how would you handle this?'

'Well, I would be giving somebody a good smack in the mouth! Give me a few moments to think about the situation.'

I smiled. She totally understands my frustration, and I think Peter would have liked to think about the answer as well.

At Eastbourne, we landed at a small airstrip. I still hadn't touched my bacon sandwich, so I gave it to Jeffrey, and we headed towards the building.

Outside there was a cab. No, no, we are not in Australia. There was a taxi waiting, and we drove to the hotel.

Once we arrived, we went up the steps of the hotel and into the foyer. We went to the reception desk, where we heard a voice. 'Michelle, what are you doing here?'

The woman would have been in her mid-50s, very attractive, with dark hair. She looked the perfect lady to manage a hotel of this quality.

'Good morning, Barbara, may I introduce you to Mr Evans.'

I put my hand out and shook hers. It was a polite business, but friendly handshake.

'And of course, you know Frank.'

She said, 'Hello Frank, perhaps we could go into my office.' We followed her. I was very impressed with the quality of the hotel and the style; you'd expect to meet the King there. We all sat in very comfortable chairs. Barbara ordered coffee and refreshments.

A well-dressed man walked in. He looked straight at Frank, who said to him, 'Good morning, James, are you keeping well?'

'Yes, thank you, yourself?'

'I'm doing very well, and enjoying myself, you know Michelle of course.'

James looked at Michelle and put his hand out and shook hers. 'It's been a long time since I've seen you.'

Michelle said, 'I'll get straight to the point James, we think you have spent enough time here learning what you need to know about running a hotel, and this one is one of the best.' She slowly glanced at Barbara. 'We know you've had the very best of training, and we very much need your expertise in our head office, there will be a little something to make it easier for you, could we say, in one week, return on the Monday?' She raised her eyebrows, that little female touch.

'Yes, I would be delighted.' James shook her hand again, but this time her hand grip was in charge.

Michelle said to Barbara, 'I have some women's business I would like to discuss; could we talk in the garden?'

'Yes, certainly.'

I watched them walk away. Michelle turned her head slightly and winked at me. I drank my coffee and enjoyed the refreshments. Soon Michelle and Barbara returned, and it was time to go.

I asked our pilot, Jeffrey, if he could fly over the chalk cliffs and the lighthouse; it brought back many good memories.

We soon arrived back at the house. Michelle and Frank got out, and we took off again for London. I arrived back at the office, where Chris asked. 'All sorted out?'

'Yes, Chris, he'll be back on Monday.'

CHAPTER 13

I opened the safe and took out the last envelope. Inside were contracts of employment. I looked at the first one. Neil Gilham, I quickly glanced through it. It still had five years to go. I put it down and picked up the next one.

Naomi Brown. I stared at it for a moment, then went back to the letter Peter had left for me, he had written Naomi Brown, not Naomi Gilham, that means they were not married when Peter was alive. Her contract also had five years to go.

The next two contracts were for the Solicitors. There were others, but I could go through them later.

'Chris, could you ask Mr Gilham to come and see me, please?' Every time I spoke to staff, it was always Mrs Gilham, why not Mr Gilham?'

There was a knock at the door, and in walked Mr Gilham, followed by Mrs Gilham. Mr Gilham said. 'Good afternoon, Sir.'

'Good afternoon.'

I looked straight at Mrs Gilham. 'Can I help you?'

Her face was stern, but her eyes twitched. 'You asked for us.'

'No, I asked for Mr Gilham, my manager, not my sales manager. Thank you, Mrs Gilham.'

She looked at her husband for some support, but he didn't give it. She looked annoyed and left, leaving the door open.

'Please sit down Neil, would you like a coffee?'

His eyebrows dropped, then he said. 'Yes please, flat white, two sugars.' He was still looking at me, he had a serious look on his face. Chris got up and closed the door, she then went and made us two coffees.

'Now Neil, I apologise for not talking to you sooner, but I've had a few problems to sort out for Peter Smith, now everything is in order. Now from your situation, is everything in order for you?'

He smiled at me. 'Yes, it is now that we have somebody in command. I'm the Manager, but I take commands from others who own this company, I now know where I stand.'

He was trying to tell me something, are others trying to manipulate his company?

'Well Neil, if we finish our coffee, we can start at the foyer and work our way up, you just talk to me, and I'll listen.'

We started down at the foyer by going first to the Reception desk, where Neil officially introduced me to the Receptionists, I shook their hands again. 'Neil, this lady is Jodie Howard, she will be working with myself and Chris.' I politely nodded to them. Then we walked over to the two ladies at the model of the tower, where Neil introduced me to the ladies, from there we went into the hairdressers shop, and Neil introduced me to the staff, at least the shop doesn't put restrictions on their customers. Next, the coffee shop, which didn't impress me one bit! The chairs and tables weren't exactly clean and they were worn out and tattered. I was introduced to a gentleman whose eyes were bloodshot and he looked very tired, he certainly didn't impress me.

Neil said. 'We lease this shop to him, without restrictions on his customers.'

What customers? There wasn't anybody there.

Neil told me. 'Our people clean the foyer, but not the shops, it is one of my problems.'

We went up to the next floor, which was the Accounts department. 'We have customers who lease or rent property, it is easier for them to come to the first floor to settle their accounts.

We went up to the next couple of floors where I was introduced to each Manager of that section, then we finally got to the legal floor. Neil introduced me to the Receptionist, I asked to see Bill Collins and she ushered us into his office.

I said. 'Good Afternoon Bill.' we shook hands. 'Bill, Michelle has three certificates for flying, one is for flying helicopters, could you register her with the company and arrange for insurance and anything else that is required. Could you also advise me if somebody is using our helicopter for their own personal use, and not for company business, where do we stand legally?'

Bill raised his eyebrows. 'Yes, I will.'

He knew what I was up to, and smiled at me. 'Catch up with you later Bill.' I nodded to him and walked out into the foyer.

The next couple of floors were the hotel. Neil introduced me to the Manager. 'This is your Manager. Ms Kela Bregu, Kela comes from Armenia. Kela, this is Mr Trevor Evans, he is the owner of this company.' She put her hand out to me, and I shook it.

She said, in very broken English, 'I'ma very pleased to meet with you.'

I replied. 'When did you meet Peter Smith?'

'Was when I was having coffee with a friend, and er, Peter walked past, as he'a knew my friend, we'a talked. He asked a lota questions about me, I 'er, answered them best I coulda. A month later my friend said to me Peter Smith wants to see you, so I go and'a see him, he givesa me this 'er position, he'a say to me, a do not give customers a piece of cake, give them 'an all of it.'

'We have people from all over the world, and you give them what they eat in their own country, they fly in, land on this building, stay in this hotel, meet with their clients and fly out, nobody else knows that they are here, it is all very private.'

Neil thanked Kela for the excellent job she had been doing. Peter was very pleased.

Kela said. 'Mrs Gilham said she wanted to change the size of the meal, then I say, e, no, she not happy.'

'You leave the meals and everything else exactly the way you're doing it.'

Kela put her thumb up in the air, and said. 'Excuse me, I er, have customers who have just arrived.'

She had heard the helicopter, and was off to meet them.

'Neil, could we have a Scotch and dry ginger together.'

'Yes, certainly.'

'In another three weeks I believe you have a four day weekend coming up.'

'Yes, we do.'

'Could you meet with me at 10 am tomorrow, in the foyer, we will solve your problem with the restaurant then. Is there anything else that troubles you?'

He knew I was setting him up, with a serious look, he looked straight into my eyes, and looked down at his glass of scotch.

'Yes, there is. Peter Smith was a great colleague of my fathers, they were very close friends, my father is at the top of a banking syndicate, and I got the job here because of Peter, I feel I've let him and my father down.' He swallowed a mouthful of his scotch, then looked straight at me. 'When Naomi first started with the company she was warm, friendly, and easy to work with, and I thought she was the one for me. Once Peter passed away, she was the one I leant on for support, that was when I met Ross Uren, who is an International Lawyer. Naomi introduced me to him. Naomi and I got married against my father's advise, we were married on a tropical island and that is where we were going to spend our honeymoon. Naomi didn't want a big Wedding.'

I put my hand out, and we shook hands, the right way, we sipped our drinks and I said. 'I will enjoy working with you Neil, and I must be honest with you, as you have been with me. Mr Smith left me a letter, in which he tells me that you do good work, and make him money, your only fault, is that sometimes you are a bully, and not always tactful. But, I also have faults. I have a problem with spelling, it has blocked me from going higher up in the management of companies, but I have given those people what they needed, and I was successful.

Neil said. 'This morning, on my computer, I had an email from Gatwick Airport, and apparently you have 20 acres of land adjacent to the airport, which they would like to acquire for additional parking, would you be interested?'

'Could you leave that with me for a moment to think about, but please keep it to yourself.'

'Now Trevor, Peter Smith has four antique cars in our car park. Naomi is using one of them, a very impressive BMW, and, as we are very short of parking spaces, I would like to put them on show in the foyer, to impress our clients, and people passing by will be able to see them through the glass windows.'

I studied his face for a moment. 'Does that mean all four?'

He grinned. 'Yes, Trevor.'

'I agree with you that they should be on show, I'll leave it in your capable hands. I know that you'll enjoy it. Now Neil, the young lady, Jodie Howard in the foyer, could you ask her to take up the position at the desk outside my office, she will act as Mrs Ayres secretary, and could you also make sure the toilet has the appropriate hand rails for her.

Neil replied. 'Between you and me, I think you made the decision to put her in that position for future training.'

'No, I want to establish a firm chain of command politically to somebody. I think you need a new car of your choosing, would you say we're both plaything the same game?'

'Yes, Trevor.'

I picked up my glass. 'One more for the road.' He grinned. I put my glass in the air and the waiter came and took it.

CHAPTER 14

The next morning at breakfast, Michelle said to me. 'Neil had an email from Gatwick Airport regarding the 20 acres of land that you own. They would like to purchase it for a car park.'

'Well, you're on the ball, aren't you, Michelle? Neil told me yesterday. What do you suggest, Michelle?'

'We make an appointment to see them.'

'Now, Michelle, they want something from us. The land to us is a nice, tidy investment; the money is tucked away, its value goes up greater than the rates. Would you suggest it would be convenient to meet with them at 2.30 pm tomorrow, at our business address, sign your name, and let them know our heliport is available for them. This way we pull the strings.' I raised my eyebrows. 'Both you and Frank can conduct the interview. We want it to work for us. If we build an eight-floor car park, it wouldn't interfere with the flights, and it will also have heavy haulage and general freight parking available. I would suggest half of the floors be for general parking, and to have offices and glass windows facing the entrance, so that they can see what is coming and going, we could lease it to them, then we would make money. What do you think about that?'

'It sounds very good, Trevor.'

'But it is only a suggestion Michelle, I will leave it up to you, and the way you handle it. Have a solicitor with you for legal advice, be polite and tactful, but hard; it is after all business. Do you have anything else for me, Michelle? Something nice and juicy.'

'Yes, we do. Somebody has been going through the accounts department's computers. Things do not tally with what is on Peter's records. When it happened, both our solicitors were with you in Australia. Our head accountant, Neville, was told to take two weeks' holiday. He had quite a number of weeks owing. The other accountant had been transferred to the hotel, so whoever had gone through the accounts was good at what they were doing. We also looked at the problems at the two factories. This is where the accounts don't make any sense according to Peter's records and the accounts today.'

Just then, Grumpy walked in the door and said good morning. He looked at me and said, 'G'day mate, how'ya going?'

I stared at him for a moment, deep in thought, then said, 'Too right, mate, she's a beauty. Come and have some good tucker. I've got a job for you to do. You've got your own car, haven't you?'

'Yes.'

'Good. Michelle will give you two addresses of warehouses in Oxted, which are next to each other. I want you to sit in your car and photograph anything that comes and goes out of the warehouses, and anything that looks out of the ordinary. June will make you some sandwiches and a flask of coffee, with a little something in it. Michelle will explain it all to you. You are now on the payroll. The game is afoot, Mr Watson.'

I heard the helicopter landing, slid back my chair and stood up and said to Michelle, '2 pm in my office.'

I winked at her, put my thumb up, and left.

CHAPTER 15

I was sitting at my desk, deep in thought, when a knock at the door startled me.

In walked Neil Gilham, followed by Jodie Howard in her wheelchair. He nodded to me and said, 'Good morning.' He turned to Chris and said, 'Good morning, Ms Ayres.' Then he turned to Jodie and said, 'Jodie, this is Chris Ayres; you will now be her secretary. I'll leave you with her.' He turned to me and said, 'See you in the foyer, Sir.' Then he left.

'Good morning, Miss Howard,' I said.

'Good morning, Sir.'

'If there is anything you need for yourself to make your life easier, or to make your work easier, please let Chris know. In this office when there's nobody else around, we use first names. Your job, where I'm concerned, is at the desk outside the door, in the foyer to this office. You need to record the name and time any visitors come, and when they leave. If you have any doubts at all, call Chris. Coffee or tea is available to you at any time in my office, or just call Margaret, and she will get it for you. If you need sandwiches or other food, Margaret will get it for you. She is the Gopher, but not our servant. See you shortly.'

I went down to the main foyer, where Neil was waiting. We walked into the restaurant. A man wearing a dirty, crappy apron walked up to us. Neil said, 'Good morning, Jim.'

Jim just looked at us. 'I know why you're here; let's get on with it. I know the lease has expired.'

'Jim, the restaurant isn't working out, so we must now close it. It isn't making anybody any money. I have a feeling, Jim, that you've got personal problems. How can we make it easier for you?'

'Yes, I've got bloody personal problems. I've got cancer and can't fight it anymore.'

'We have our own van and workforce, tell us where to take everything,' Neil replied.

I put my hand on Neil's shoulder, letting him know I agreed.

Jim said, 'I'll have to sell it all.'

Neil looked him straight in the eye. 'I'll handle it all for you. I've got a good friend who buys and sells.'

'If there are any problems, let us know so that we can fix them before they get too big,' I added. Then I shook his hand. Neil did the same.

We walked out of the restaurant. I didn't feel it was right; I turned around and gestured to him with my hand. 'Any problems!' and nodded, he nodded back.

As we walked past the receptionists, I said. 'Good morning, ladies.' They all said, 'Good morning, Sir.'

Before we go any further, Neil, the lady who runs the restaurant across the road is Bill's sister-in-law, Lesley.'

He looked at me and raised his eyebrows. We walked across the road and into her restaurant. Most of the tables were full. Lesley, with a smile on her face, said, 'Good morning gentlemen, a table for two?'

I said, 'Lesley, could we speak business first?'

Her eyes flickered back and forwards at us. 'Yes, the table over there in the corner.' She looked at me. 'You drink a flat white with two sugars.'

'Yes, thank you.'

Neil said, 'The same for me, thank you.'

We sat down at the table. Lesley brought out three coffees and sat down at the table with us.

'Lesley, you know who I am, and this is Neil Gilham, my manager. We have a vacant restaurant in our main foyer. Would you like to take it over? You wouldn't be paying a lease.' I saw her eyes flinch, then I said, 'There is a catch. I have staff running my business, they need to be fed good food and good coffee. I need them to be content, but I don't want them sitting in your restaurant all day. So, could they email you, or call in first thing in the morning and order their egg and bacon sandwiches and coffee? How they pay is up to you. You can give them daily credit, which they could pay every week. One of your staff could deliver the food to whichever department they are in. I will let nobody take advantage of you. Business is business. There is a four-day weekend coming up. Could you move in then, and anybody in the street can use your restaurant, you may put up a sign outside to say that is where you are moving to.' I put my hand out. 'Is that a deal?'

Lesley had tears in her eyes. 'Yes, yes, how could anybody refuse an offer like that?'

'Neil will have our people put it all in writing, and our legal team will sort out any minor problems. One other thing, you employ your own staff. Neil will arrange for the restaurant to be painted and the kitchen to be put back into order. I think that just about covers everything.'

Neil and I shook hands with Lesley. 'We're looking for an excuse to sample your coffee.' I grinned at her.

Lesley replied, 'Would you excuse me, please, gentlemen? I have to go to the bathroom to compose myself; this wouldn't look good in front of the customers.'

'While we have a moment, Neil. I've got to train Michelle, so when you told me the airport wanted to purchase twenty acres of land, she arranged for a meeting in my office at 2 pm to talk it over. If you want to be there, it's up to you, but I need a copy of the title for that piece of land, and make sure it's not landlocked.'

'Yes, I would like to be there,' he said.

'And be discreet,' I said.

'No worries. Now, my little problem, Trevor, is the keys to the antique cars.'

'I'll look in the safe in my office, Neil.'

Just then, two plates of delicious-looking sponge cake ladened with fresh whipped cream, ice cream and fruit turned up in front of us. A lady with a big grin on her face was standing alongside us.

I got back to the office and looked at the watch that Jackie had bought for me. I felt a twinge of loneliness. It was 11.45 am. 'Chris, could you phone Neville, our head accountant, and ask him to come up and see me, please?'

Margaret brought me a cup of coffee and asked whether I would like something to eat. I patted my stomach. 'Thank you very much, Margaret, but I think there's enough in there already.'

I looked down at my desk. Chris had put paperwork there for me to read. There was a gold pen on top of the papers. Just then, there was a knock at the door, and Neville walked in. He was just about to say good morning to me when Chris's voice boomed out. 'Look what the wind blows in when you leave the door open!'

Neville retorted, 'I thought we had gotten rid of you. You're a head-ache! But when you disappeared, I missed you. When you were here, everything was in order. I knew exactly where I stood, and I'm still lost. Good morning, Sir.'

I stood up and shook his hand. 'I'm sorry I haven't seen you earlier, but I needed to sort out a few things for Peter. Your companion will be back on Monday. Let's say he's done some training at a hotel. Now Neville, do you have any problems you would like to discuss? Oh, and call me Trevor.'

'Yes, Trevor, I have some problems. When I was on holiday, somebody went through my computer and backup system. Whoever it was, he or she is good at what they do. They've been through my desk and filing cabinet also, and I don't know who.' He was angry and frustrated.

'Neville, Peter had a backup system, so we can fix your problem.' Then I saw Neville staring at the gold pen, which was sitting on my papers.

'Trevor, where did you get that pen?'

'Ross Uren handed it to me to sign some papers. I kept it to make a statement. I will sign the papers when I know what they are for.'

He looked at me seriously. 'Could you read what's written on the pen?'

I put my glasses on and picked up the pen, turning it over so that I could see the inscription.

Neville said, 'I will tell you what it says. *From Winnie in gratitude for the support you gave me during the dark years. PM.* My father's name was Peter Marshall, and that pen was in the top drawer of my desk. When I got back, it was gone!'

I had noticed the gold mark on it. So, Mr Uren couldn't resist picking it up and putting it in his pocket. That answers the question. I handed the pen back to Neville.

'Now, back to Michelle; she will see you this afternoon or first thing in the morning. I will let you know; she will sort out some of your problems for you, especially your records and computer. Now, Peter Smith has left me lots of notes, and he tells me you're #1, and you will always watch my back! Now, are there any other problems I can help you with?'

'Yes, get Mrs Gilham off my back!'

'Chris, could you please get Mrs Gilham on the phone for me?' She pushed a button on her desk. I picked up the phone. 'Good afternoon, Trevor Evans here. Could you please give me Mrs Gilham?' There was a slight pause.

'She's at a meeting at the moment, Sir.'

'Give the phone to her! You ever say that to me again, and you will be looking for another job! You work for me, not Mrs Gilham!'

Then a voice said, 'How can I help you?'

'Yes, Mrs Gilham. My head accountant answers only to me and my general manager; nobody else. Do you understand?'

Silence says a lot. 'Yes, Sir, thank you,' she replied. I hung up.

With a great big grin, Neville said, 'Thank you, Trevor.'

I looked at my watch. 'We have time, coffee or tea, Neville?'

'Tea, milk and sugar, please.' I said out loud.

'Fancy are you?' a voice came back.

'Yes, I'm awake, one flat white. One tea with milk and sugar, please.'

The voice came back. 'In mugs?'

'This office hasn't changed one bit. Peter is still here,' Neville said.

Chris said the same. 'System 12 bells, and all's well.'

'Now, Neville, the gentleman running the restaurant in the foyer is leaving. Let's just say he's all paid up. We will have new people taking over the restaurant. They are from across the road and will move in during the four-day long weekend. They don't have a lease with us; the legal department will sort it all out, and they will employ their own staff and pay for their gas, electricity and water. None of their utilities are freebies. Chris, do you have any questions for our colleague here?'

'Yes, I do, because he's such a lovely man and so generous, he's going to let me have a fuel card!'

Neville replied with, 'Some people push the boundaries, don't they, Trevor? Just because they've got friends in high places. Yes Mum, in about three weeks.'

'Thank you, Neville darling!'

To which Neville gallantly replied, 'Yes, dear, no, dear, anything else, dear?'

'No, you are dismissed!'

'Trevor, she always gets the last word.'

As we finished our drinks, there was a knock on the door, and in walked Michelle and Frank. Michelle saw Neville and shouted out, 'Uncle Neville!' She put her arms around him and kissed him on the cheek.

He smiled at her warmly. 'Michelle, from now on, while you are in this building, I cannot be Uncle Neville, because I believe that I'll be working for you and Peter, and it won't look good where we are here. But elsewhere I'll still chase you around the garden!'

'You'll always be Uncle Neville to me, and Grumpy will always be Uncle Grumpy to me,' Michelle said.

'Now, you two, we must get back to business. Michelle, I want you and Frank to work with Neville to put everything in his office back to normal. I would also like you to work back; it's very important to me and Neville. Tomorrow, if you want Frank back with you in your little cubby, that's quite alright with me. The chopper is Neville's to use; we use the word chopper in Australia.'

'See you in my office later, Ms Smith,' Neville said. Michelle frowned, and Neville left the office.

'Michelle, I've asked Neil to sit in on the next meeting, so he knows what's going on. He is your man, not Naomi's'.

'Is it alright if Margaret and I sort out some business elsewhere?' Chris said.

'Yes, Chris, feel free.'

She gave me a little curtsy. 'Come on, Margaret, we have something else to do.' And they were off.

'Frank, could you go and greet our guests, please?' He was off as well.

There was another knock at the door, and Neil walked in, we could hear the helicopter. 'Neil, could you make both of us a drink, please?'

Saying nothing, he went straight to the bar. 'Michelle, could you sit at Peter's desk?'

I walked over and sat at Chris's desk. Neil put the two glasses down on Chris's desk and drew up another chair for himself. He took a pen out of his top pocket, picked up one of Chris's notepads, and he was ready. He put his hand into his inside pocket, two out two pieces of paper. One was the title to the land; he gave it to me. I studied it, then looked at Neil. 'It's landlocked! There's no access to it!'

He grinned and handed me the second piece of paper, saying, 'Peter was always one step ahead.'

I read the second piece of paper. It went back to when the airport was first built. There was a road alongside the fence. It was a public road, which gave access to Peter's land. This paper gave him the right to enter and leave anytime he wished, using McCloud Road. It had figures informing us exactly where it was, and all the legal jargon that goes with such a document.

I walked over to Michelle and put the two documents down in front of her. 'Don't let them know you've got this information yet; keep it as a draw card until the end.'

There was a knock at the door; Frank came in with three gentlemen behind him. He introduced all of us to them; we shook hands but didn't say what positions we had in the company. It wasn't exactly polite but was tactically convenient.

Michelle said, 'Welcome, gentlemen, please sit down. I assume you had a pleasant flight in our helicopter?'

One of the men leaned forward. 'Yes, it's not very often we fly over the city and land on top of a building.'

'Now, gentlemen, you wish to purchase some land from us?'

The same man answered. 'Yes, we do. We are looking towards the future, and parking is going to be the problem, and, I must admit, your land is situated exactly in the right place.'

Michelle replied. 'Yes, it is. Now, every organisation must have a little money tucked away for a rainy day, so what makes you think we would part with the land?'

'Well, it would be in the public interest and in looking after their welfare.'

Michelle then said, 'If we sold everything off in the public interest, we would lose our security to survive a rainy day. Gentlemen, I respectfully ask you to remember this is business, and that piece of land is very valuable to us as an investment; it is there for our future. I could make another suggestion if you wish.'

The three men glanced at each other and communicated just with eye movements.

The same man as before said, 'Yes, we are open for suggestions.'

'Well gentlemen, what if we were to build an eight-storey car park, with additional parking for large transport and heavy haulage on the ground floor, and on the 2nd floor, put in an office with windows, so that you could see who is coming and going, and lease it to you. We would not be putting in a fuel bowser; it would be too complicated and costly, but if you wish, you could put in surface fuel tanks. This could be discussed further, but I know you have a service station very close, which could be used by your customers.'

The three men glanced at each other. One of the other men asked, 'May we discuss this in private, please?'

Michelle replied. 'Yes, if you would like to go up to the day room, it would be private there.'

The three men left and went to the day room.

Michelle handed Frank a piece of paper. 'Could you get three copies, please?' He was just returning when the three men came back and sat down.

'Ms Smith, we have a slight problem here. Your land is landlocked, so you cannot sell it to anybody else in the near future.'

Michelle stared at him for just a moment, then said, 'Frank.'

Frank handed each man a copy of the paper, which they read.

One of the men said to his colleague, 'You have not done your homework!'

To which his colleague replied. 'I knew of this, but it was a long time ago. I thought nobody would know.'

The first spokesman said, 'I don't think I would like to play chess with you. We agree to your terms. You build it, and we will lease it from you if our architects can work with your architects.'

Michelle replied, 'I don't see why not. But we would like four parking spaces for our company cars, but only when we're in transit.'

'I agree, and so do my colleagues.'

Neil said, 'I will have a contract typed up so that you can sign it off.' He got up and left.

Michelle said, 'Would you gentlemen like some drinks and something to eat?'

To which they all replied. 'Yes, we would enjoy that, thank you.'

Michelle ushered them to the lift. 'Our restaurant is on the top floor.'

CHAPTER 16

I sat thinking that went extremely well. But what is my next problem? I glanced at the building site next door. Where does the company stand financially with the Tower? Where are we involved and how deep? I don't like it, and I wondered if there were any more papers in the safe. I got up and went to the safe and opened it. Inside there was a cigar box, which I took out and opened. There were keys inside, with tags on them. I read the first one – 1949 Rolls-Royce Silver Dawn. The second one said 1948 Jaguar Mark V, the third, 1946 Triumph Roadster, and the last one, 1956 BMW. I stared at them for a moment, and wondered just how Naomi was driving the BMW, when I had the keys? I put them all back into the cigar box.

I took out a large envelope, which had DUBAI CONTRACT written on the front. I opened it, took out a piece of paper and read it. Apparently, Peter had owned the land on which the tower was being built. He was leasing the land to a company in Dubai. I stared at it for a moment. What was Peter's backup? What if they failed to pay the lease? What would he own? Where would it leave him? He always had a backup plan. I put the papers back into the safe and closed the door. I had better go to the restaurant and be polite.

To my surprise, when I got out of the lift at the restaurant, I saw Ross Uren with two other gentlemen. He looked straight at me; he looked guilty. I said, 'Good afternoon, Mr Uren. What brings you to the hotel? Are you staying here?'

Mrs Bregu, the hotel's manager, said, 'No, they have only been here for a meal.'

One of the men said, 'It was a damn good meal too.' By the way he spoke, I knew he was a Cockney.

I put my hand out. 'I am Trevor Evans, and I own this business. Mrs Bregu, has Mr Uren paid his bill?'

To which she replied, 'No, he hasn't. Mrs Gilham said he could eat here anytime for free.'

'That isn't correct,' I answered. 'Only people staying at this hotel, or my management team who are with invited clients, can eat here for free.'

One of the men, who wore a very chunky gold necklace and had rings on most of his pudgy fingers, said, 'My name is Freddie. I have a nightclub in Soho. Does Ross Uren have anything to do with this company?'

'No, he does not,' I replied.

The man turned to Ross. 'What cock and bull stories have you been telling me? Now, Mr Evans, anytime you want a good night out, come down to my club. It's called Freddie's. We'll give you a good time, and my girls will look after you.'

'Whereabouts in London do you come from, Freddie? You talk just like my father, and he came from Blackfriars.'

Freddie said, 'Well, I never! That's where I come from. Rose Street. You have an Australian accent; your father wouldn't have been Les, who had a twin brother Arthur?'

'Yes, he was.'

'Well, I never! You wouldn't believe it. My dad, who was Bill, kept the rabbits, bloody, stinking things they were.'

I put my hand out again. 'So, we are related.' He shook my hand. I thought it was going to fall off.

'Catch up with you later,' he said. 'Now Ross, you've been telling me porky pies, so we have a bit of talking to do.'

He turned to the other man, who I guessed was his minder. 'Pay the bill.' The man took a bundle of notes out of his inside pocket and paid the bill.

Freddie said, 'See you later, Trev. Come on, Ross, we have a bit of business to get sorted.'

The lift doors opened, and out walked Neil, looking surprised. The three men got into the lift, and they were gone. Neil looked at me, confused. 'That was Freddie and Ross.'

'Yes, they thought they were going to have a free lunch,' I said.

'Don't ever cross Freddie. That big guy with him sorts out people very well.'

We went into the dining room and joined our guests. We signed the papers, and, as my dad would say, *everything was hunky-dory, all tied up with a neat bow.* He also said to me, *'Don't mess with a Cockney.'*

As we were leaving, I said to Neil, 'See you in the carpark at 10 am tomorrow. Could you let Bill know? I want him to be there also, with any additional information he has about next door's building. I put my hand on his shoulder. 'Have a good night, Neil.'

CHAPTER 17

At breakfast the next morning, I said to Michelle, 'Would you like to fly into town with me this morning?'

'Yes, Frank and I would love to, Trevor. Neil put one more item on the contract for the airport. He suggested we wire up the building for electric cars. They will put the chargers on the stands themselves.'

I winked at her. 'Does that mean we can charge all our cars?'

She grinned. 'Not my car, I like fossil fuel!'

Grumpy walked in the door saying good morning to everyone. He put his hand on my shoulder and said, 'I put my trilby hat, dark glasses, camera and trench coat on my expense account, is that okay, boss?'

'Grumpy, I've got an Akubra hat, a Driza-Bone coat and boots at home. I'll get them sent over, then you can take yours back to the shop. Just don't take them out of the boxes.'

Grumpy gave me a nudge with his elbow, and sat down, ready for his breakfast.

Michelle said, 'Could you get me a saddle as well, one of those big stockman ones? I could use it!'

I asked Grumpy for a report on the previous day's workings.

'Well, there are a lot of things coming and going from the two factories. Vans turned up early in the morning; they appeared to be fully loaded with goods. At 6 am, two buses turned up; quite a few of what looked like migrant women got off, and I've come here for my breakfast, sandwiches and a thermos, then I'm going back. Everything's on film.' He handed me the first film. 'Now, Trevor, there's another car watching the factories as well.'

I stared at him for a moment. 'June, do you think Grumpy could use your car today as a precaution?'

'No, Trevor, I will drive my car, and Grumpy will be my passenger. You've never seen Grumpy drive, have you?'

Grumpy said, 'I love you too. Do you have two thermoses? You wouldn't want mine.'

June scowled at him. The back door opened, and Chris walked in. 'Good morning, folks.' As she passed June, she put a hand on her shoulder, then sat down.

'Trevor, do you remember when Naomi left the door open?'

'Yes, I do.'

'Well, when I went to close it, she was standing just around the corner; I could see her elbow.'

'Very interesting, Chris, I will remember that. June, we know who went through the computers. He left the evidence. He took a gold pen out of Neville's desk.' She looked at me and smiled.

Michelle said, 'Trevor, it's Friday today, and I want to work on the computers on Saturday and Sunday with Frank and another colleague of mine from university. His name is Ronald, and he is a wizard with computers. I know he can fix Neville's computer and restore Peter's computer information, and put it into Neville's, but I would also like Neville to be there. I believe it's his privacy. Today I want to go through everything in his department with him, so that we don't miss anything.'

I said nothing, just picked up my coffee and sipped it, thinking, *she's doing well, Peter, isn't she?* I could hear the helicopter landing. 'Time to go, ladies and gentlemen.'

Frank turned up from nowhere, saying, 'But I haven't had breakfast yet.'

As she was getting up from the table, Michelle looked at him with a cheeky grin, saying, 'The early bird catches the worm. Come on, Frank, when we're in the helicopter, I'll fill you in on what's going on.'

Once we arrived at our building, I went to my office and sat down. What do I do? Do I shut down the stores going into the two factories? Yes, but apparently, it's on Thursday afternoons that they pick them up, so that they are delivered early Friday morning, fewer people around. But I've got to let the managers of the other factories know. I haven't met them yet.

'Chris, could you ask the two managers from our factories and their seconds to meet me here on Saturday morning? We will invite them and their wives out to lunch, and so there are no arguments, you and June will be there as well. I will also inform the hotel of the booking.'

Chris said, 'Margaret is moving into her new apartment on the long weekend, and I'm going to help her.'

'Chris, is there anything you need to make it easier?'

'No, it's all arranged.'

'Those papers on my desk, Chris, I assume they are the invoices for things to be paid. I slowly went through them, signing them. One was for the lease of her car; another was for Neil Gilham's car.' There was a knock at the door, and in burst Margaret. She was all hyped up.

'Chris, I have just been to see my new apartment. It's beautiful. I want to discuss with you where I put my furniture.' She clapped her hands together. 'I'm so excited; I never dreamed I would have my own home.' She walked over to me and kissed me on the cheek. 'Thank you, Trevor.' She turned and cuddled Chris; she had tears in her eyes.

I said, 'Ladies, where is my coffee?' They laughed and said, 'In the kitchen,' and they disappeared.

I finished signing the papers and sat there for a while thinking of what Jackie was doing now and what the children were up to. I hope

Charlie is looking after her. I do miss Australia. I looked at my watch, nearly time for my next meeting. I kissed my watch, thinking of Jackie. Margaret brought me my coffee, which I slowly sipped. I picked up the sugar bowl and walked towards the door. The two girls were chatting about the apartment; they wouldn't even know I had left.

I went to the lift and pressed the basement button. The carpark was full of cars on all four floors. Neil was there with another man, waiting for me.

Neil introduced us. 'Jock, this is Mr Evans. Mr Evans, this is Jock McPhee. Peter used to call him his headache. He's been with Peter for 30 years. Peter wanted to move him up in the company, but Jock loves the carpark; that's why he called him a headache.'

Jock replied to this by saying, 'This is my patch. I know where I stand here, and I'm quite content.'

I shook his hand. 'When nobody's around, my name is Trevor. Now, Neil suggests we put the antique cars in the foyer. Here are the keys. One thing that puzzles me. Naomi is driving the BMW. How did she get the key?'

'She had a locksmith change the lock and ignition, and make new keys,' Jock replied.

'Do you have a receipt for that?'

'Yes, I do, and I have the registration plate.'

'How do we get into that car now?'

'Peter Smith insisted that everybody who had a hire car leave the keys on a hook in my office. Naomi leaves both her car keys in my office on that hook.'

'You said both car keys?'

'Yes, she has a Mercedes station wagon as well.'

'Okay, move all four cars into the foyer today.' I paused for a few moments.

'Do you know where the original locks are?'

'Yes, I do. They're in my office.'

'You're a good man, Jock. I like the way you do things. Could you please have a locksmith replace them after the cars have been put in the foyer, and could you let Neil drive them into the foyer? It isn't favouritism; it's politics. Now, I need Neil this morning; will this afternoon be alright?'

'Yes, Trevor, it will take me that long to sort things out.'

'Good, is there anything else I can help you with?'

'Yes, if you could follow me.' We went up to a very large cupboard, which he opened, switched on the light. In it there was a motorbike, along with a leather jacket, pants, gloves, helmet and boots. 'These were Peter Smith's. He used to come down and take the bike for a ride now and then. He said it helped clear his mind and sort out his problems.' The motorbike was an Arial Foursquare Motorbike 1931, designed by Edward Turner. 'Would you like me to put this in the foyer as well?'

'Yes, Jock, I would.'

'Now Trevor, I have a glass cabinet in the storeroom; could I put his leather gear in that glass cabinet?'

I looked at Jock. 'Good suggestion.' I put my hand out and shook his. 'Now, you two go have some fun.' I turned around, got into the lift and went back up to my office.

Whilst I had been away, Naomi had walked into my office and asked Chris where I was.

Chris said to her, 'Where is who?'

In a very arrogant voice. Naomi replied, 'Mr Evans, you fool.'

Chris, trying to compose herself, said, 'I don't know; he didn't tell me. The phone call yesterday from him wasn't.' She stopped herself. She knew she was losing her cool.

Naomi said, 'Mr Evans has been here for quite a few days, and I haven't had a meeting with him yet. I'm very busy, could you ask my secretary when it's convenient for me to have a meeting with him?'

Chris was enjoying this. 'Exactly who is him?'

'Mr Evans! Now where are the papers for me to sign to run this company?'

Chris thought to herself. Arrogant bitch! 'Mr Evans has signed all the invoices to run this company; it is his company. If I'm wrong, please let me know.'

Naomi scowled at Chris and said, 'I thought I'd got rid of you!'

Chris composed herself and whispered to herself *Your day's coming*. Naomi turned around and walked out of the office, leaving the door open. As she went down in one lift, I came up in the other.

Jody said, 'A woman came up before. She walked right past me without even looking at me. She went into your office. I believe it was Mrs Gilham. She came back, leaving the door open. She didn't look at me and went back to the lifts.'

'Thank you, Jody, for letting me know.'

I went into the office and closed the door. I swear I could see steam coming out of Chris's ears. She also seemed to be gritting her teeth. I stayed with Chris for just a moment. 'Chris, let's say you've had the last word. The BMW will be on show in the foyer with the rest of the cars and the motorbike.'

She looked at me for a moment and said, 'Could you please excuse me for a moment? I have to go to the ladies' room.' I could hear her laughing as she walked away.

I went back to the safe and opened it. I took out another large envelope, which had DUBAI written on the front. I closed the safe door and went back to my desk, where I inspected the documents from the envelope. There were six of them relating to the ownership of the land next door. To me, they were all confusing. The dates went back to 1947, just after the war had finished. They talked about finances and bridging loans. Others referred to the City of London. There were other documents which I didn't understand.

CHAPTER 18

There was a knock on the office door, and Neil Gilham walked in. He looked very pleased with himself.

'Good morning, Neil. You look like the bird who has caught a big worm.'

'Trevor, I have just talked to Naomi, or should I say Naomi spoke to me. She asked me what I had said to Freddie in the restaurant yesterday.' I grinned. 'I asked him to pay the bill! Freddie introduced himself to me and asked me how Ross was involved with the company, and I told him he wasn't involved at all. I got the impression Freddie wasn't pleased,' Neil said with a big grin on his face. 'And this is the good part. Ross Uren spent the night in the hospital. They were concerned about his kidneys and a few minor bruises. Trevor, the only way I can explain it is that he must have tripped over a matchstick. Did Freddie help him up? Enough said.'

Just as Bill walked in the door, he said, 'Good morning, all.' He turned to Chris. 'What are you looking so happy about?'

'Bill, it's such a lovely day; the weather is perfect, in fact, it couldn't be any better.'

Bill looked at her, puzzled. He was wondering what she was trying to say.

Chris said, 'Three coffees?'

I replied, 'Yes, please, Chris. Now, gentlemen, if you could both bring your chairs closer to my desk. I want to know everything about the tower next door, not the figures, just the general information.'

Bill replied first. 'Trevor, I believe I should start from the beginning about what we know. At the end of the war, London was in big trouble, and the government needed help for public housing. Money was the problem. Peter had friends high up and spoke with them, and they came up with a plan. They formed a business committee. The land on which the tower is being built was bombed out, so they had it cleared, and put prefab houses on it. Quick fix for a housing problem. Then they started building high-rise buildings and leased them out to the government. Peter owned four of them as well as the land under the construction site next door. How he acquired the land, I don't know. He was a very astute businessman. Favours for favours. The government didn't argue as it solved their problem quickly. It was also the government who approached Peter on behalf of the Dubai people. Once again, the government needed housing and facilities for workers within the city. They actually needed a mini-city within a city, incorporating shopping centres, medical facilities, swimming pools, gymnasiums, everything a city has. This is the government's answer to solving a problem. By the time it's built, the lease will be dissolved in the profits. Everything Peter did, though, had a back-up plan. I believe it will come to light in the near future.'

I sat thinking for a moment. I couldn't find any questions to ask. 'Neil, do you have anything to add?'

'No, I think Bill has covered it all.'

'Neil, do you know anything about a radio tower on the building?'

'Well, Trevor, there was a rumour going around about a radio tower or communications tower being built on top of the building, but it was just a rumour.'

Bill said, 'Peter had a lot going on in his mind, which he kept to himself. I am the lawyer for this company, and I don't work for anyone else outside of this company. Peter concentrated on leasing property, factories, warehouses, apartments and many other types of leases. He could always buy and let go. He even had some canal barges leased out. The greater part of our work is receiving payments from these leased properties. From Peter's point of view, it was easy and clean, and it gave him the opportunity to wheel and deal.' He chuckled. 'He would say to me, *I bought that company — a good buy. Now I will sell that company, and it will pay for what I've just bought, and I've made a profit!*'

I sat there thinking about it all and sipping my coffee. 'Neil, he must have had a lot of tentacles spread out.'

'He certainly did,' Neil replied.

Bill asked me. 'Have we sorted things out for you?'

'Yes, in a way that I can understand, simple. So, I have the basics now. The finance part would go in one ear and out the other.'

Bill laughed. 'I'm a lawyer. I've got all the degrees, and the same thing happens to me — in one ear and out the other.'

'Thank you, gentlemen, for coming up and putting me in the picture. Bill, Neil is putting the four antique cars on show in the foyer, along with Peter's motorbike. Yes, the BMW as well!'

Bill raised his eyebrows. 'Trevor, Naomi has asked me to register the BMW in her name. I couldn't do that, but I could re-register it in Michelle's name because she is a Smith.'

Neil looked at Chris, and they both burst out laughing. I said to Neil, 'Take the plates off of the BMW and give them to Bill.'

Neil pushed his chair back, saying, 'I'll do that right away,' and he left the room.

CHAPTER 19

Chris's phone rang. She picked up the receiver and said, 'Hello. Yes, a man called Freddie. I'll ask him now. Trevor, there is a man by the name of Freddie in the foyer. He has another man with him as well; can you see them?'

I grinned and thought, another wheeler and dealer. Be careful Trevor. 'Yes, Chris, send them up.'

I looked at my watch. 12.30 pm.

Bill said, 'I will leave you with it all.' He was grinning.

Chris's phone rang again, and Jody informed her that Mr Freddie and an associate were here to see me.

I got up, walked over to the door and opened it.

Freddie said, 'How are you, me old cock and sparrow?'

'Doing well Freddie, come in.' I shook his hand and put my hand out to his colleague.

Freddie said, 'This is Jack.'

I shook his hand. 'Come in and sit down in the armchairs. How can I help you, Freddie?'

'Well, I want to put the record straight about Naomi. You and I are Cockneys, where everything has to be on the slide.'

I looked at my watch. 'How about lunch, Freddie? Then we can talk.' Jack's eyes lit up, and so did Freddie's.

We went up to the restaurant and found a table next to the window. We all ordered our meals and drinks.

'Now, Freddie, you wanted to talk about Naomi?'

'Yes, Naomi was one of my girls. She was just sixteen when she started working for me. She had been abandoned by her mother when she was eight years old and left to fend for herself on the streets. God only knows how the slimy ratbags treated her. The authorities eventually picked her up. That's when Ross Uren got involved. He was just a young lawyer then. Naomi was placed into care.'

'Like many of the young girls, my club is a magnet, especially when they have nowhere else to go. When they are there, they are with others like themselves. You can help one or two of them but unfortunately not all of them. They call me Pop. Naomi started by picking up glasses, cleaning the ***** off the floor and all the other unpleasant jobs. When she got of age, she started working behind the bar, but by then she had gotten into trouble with the fuzz. Ross was always there to get her out of trouble, and that's when I realised they were living together. It wasn't my problem; it was their private life. I know in a way I was using her, but Ross was grooming her to look after his mates, let's say in sleezy places. The next thing I knew, she was working for Peter Smith. I thought made it, that she'd got out of the rat race. I didn't realise then, as I do now, that Ross was still grooming her to take him to higher places, and he made his move when Peter Smith died. He thought you were going to be a pushover! He didn't realise you had lived the hard way and become very streetwise in Australia, with your own company. On the day you arrived, when you put him back in his place, that was priceless. As one Cockney to another, could you please look after my girl, Naomi?'

'Freddie, I will do my best,' I said.

Our meals arrived, and we sat chatting. I learned a lot more about Freddie, and I found a new respect for him. He was doing his part in society; you could say the Law of the Jungle. Jack said he wanted to go to the toilet, and he got up. I looked at the four large empty glasses in front of him. I certainly couldn't drink four pints of beer!

Freddie continued, 'I had a boxing troupe in the old days and a gym. Jack was the best. He made us all good money by working around the clubs, but he got a punch in the head, the wrong way, and spent two months in hospital. He never really recovered. He's like a son to me. He's always beside me and never questions me when I ask him to do something; he just does it.'

Jack came back and sat down. Two men from another table got up and walked over to us. One of them said, 'I don't mean to be forward, but did you used to be the bruiser?'

Jack stood up and put his hand out. 'Yes, I was.'

'You were the best; you were like lightning,' the man replied.

The other man said, 'When you fought Big Daddy, he was in trouble. You hit him, and he staggered back, totally off guard. Then the referee stepped in between you both to stop the fight, but he got in the way of your next punch, and you put him down on his backside.'

Jack was laughing, and so was Freddie. Jack said, 'I didn't win that fight; the referee stopped it. Big Daddy used to be like a tank, unstoppable.'

The two men went back to their seats. Jack looked so happy, he was a celebrity again.

Freddie looked at his watch. 'Trevor, you'll have to excuse us. I've gotta get back to the club. It's like a baby; you can never really leave it. Thanks for the chat, something you say in Australia. You're a true-blue mate.' They both left.

CHAPTER 20

I went back to my office and opened the safe again. I took out some more of the papers and put them on my desk. Then I thought to myself, don't leave the safe door open, so I went back, and closed it.

The first piece of paper had a sketch of the tower and a figure written underneath it, nothing more. I stared at it. What was Peter trying to say? The figure was not the cost of the entire project; it was too low. He had written the figure at the bottom of the paper, not at the top. If I were doodling with a pencil on a piece of paper and thinking about the tower, I would probably just sketch the tower. Then, if I were thinking about the price… but of what? Peter owns the land, so is that the value he put on the land, or has he left me another piece of information? I think so. The next piece of paper referred to the steam yacht. It had information about her construction, length, with sizes, a diagram of her out of the water with blocks underneath the keel and where to place them and the measurements.

The next three pieces of paper were clipped together. On the top one was a note to me. *Trevor, on my computer at home there is all the information you need to know for Michelle to take over the company, when you think she's ready. The password is ready. I have left the information for our lawyer*

Bill; it has all been legally sorted out. I hope you are enjoying the game. Buy and sell and stay independent from the rat race.

I put all the papers back into the safe and locked the door. I thought of going home. 'Chris, I'm going to find Michelle and go home.'

We got home and had an early dinner. All I really wanted was bed.

CHAPTER 21

The next morning, I opened my eyes. The bed was so warm and comfortable. I wanted to sleep in, but when I rolled over, I saw the curtains had been drawn. I looked out at the garden through the little leadlight windows. This was so different from Australia. The soft greens of the leaves, even the colours of the flowers, seemed brighter. The blackbirds were singing away, and I could hear the pigeons cooing to each other. A dog was barking. It was an excited bark, as though somebody was playing with it. It reminded me of Charlie; he barked like that when he was going out for a walk with Jackie.

Saturday morning, another meeting. I swung my legs over the edge of the bed and saw that my clean clothes had been laid out for me. June must have also opened the curtains. I showered and got dressed.

I went down for breakfast. Grumpy was already there, sitting next to Chris. They both looked up. Grumpy said, 'Slept in Trevor?'

'Yes, I did, and I could have slept in longer.'

Grumpy gave a small chuckle. 'Yesterday was very interesting. The one they called Barbie Doll and another fellow; I've seen him before but don't know where. He had a walking stick and leaned on it heavily, and Barbie Doll helped him to walk. Anyway, they went into the factory. Only Barbie Doll came back out, got into a Mercedes station wagon and left. Next, a bus turned up, and women with headdresses, and black clothes got off and went into the factory. Barbie Doll had been there the day before.

'Others turned up in their cars, dressed just like you and me. The other car was also there again, watching. I got some more good photos during the day. In the afternoon, Barbie Doll turned up, picked up the man with the walking stick, and drove off. Then the bus turned up, and the women came out of the factory, got back on the bus, and it drove off. I got some good photos of that as well. I followed some of the others. They left their cars at a pub where I used to drink.

'I went into the pub and got a conversation going by giving them the impression that I was looking for work. They started talking about their work. Cash in hand every day. They were rewinding armatures, pulling computers and photocopiers apart, looking for spare parts, and little bits of gold and silver. No shortage of work. Just turn up Monday morning. The other factory does the same, and the leftover rubbish is burnt in the furnace. It's a bloody sweatshop taking advantage of people.' Grumpy handed me the photos.

'Grumpy, did the other car follow you to the pub?'

'Yes, it did, but they never came into the pub, and when I left, they had gone. Trevor, what are you doing on Sunday?'

'I'm going to rest and clear my mind. Everything is moving too fast.'

'Well, Trevor, how about we take the old girl up the river, and meet an old friend of ours? We can have lunch at his pub.'

June's voice burst out. 'Yes, that's what we're going to do, have lunch with the Barrow boy, and you're coming as well, Chris. I won't take no for an answer.'

The look on Chris's face made me laugh. She couldn't argue.

'Why do you call him the Barrow boy?' I asked.

'He was a Barrow boy in Petticoat Lane,' June answered.

Grumpy said, 'He's got the slipway that we rebuilt the steam yacht in.'

'Does that mean I don't have to wear a collar and tie?' I asked.

'Yes, Trevor. You can wear a T-shirt, pair of shorts and thongs on your feet and carry an Esky, and you will be a real Dinky-dye Aussie again.'

Just then, Michelle walked in wearing her dressing gown. 'Michelle, I've got a meeting this morning with the factory managers. Then we're having lunch. Would you like to attend the meeting?'

'No thank you, Trevor, we have too much work to do, sorting out the information on the computers. Frank wanted to go to the footy today, and I remembered what you said about being the captain of the ship, so I said no. What I already know from what we have found out so far makes me furious. They thought they could just take over the company. I want to put them back in their place!'

Just then I heard the helicopter. 'Michelle, you can be angry and frustrated, but at the same time you have to be in control of yourself. Study the chessboard, be sure of your next move and stay in command. Do you have a backup plan ready? I believe you're already in command, and I'm enjoying watching you play the game.'

As I walked past June, I put my hand on her shoulder and then kept walking, whilst saying to everyone, 'Have a good day.' I put my thumb up in the air to Grumpy and left. Once I got to the helicopter, I asked Joe, the pilot. 'You have a young family, don't you?'

Joe replied, 'Yes, Sir, I do.'

'Well, I'll get a lift back with one of the others this afternoon. You enjoy some time with your family.'

'Thank you, Sir.'

CHAPTER 22

After we landed, I went down to the foyer to look at the antique cars. I liked the way they had placed them at a slight angle to each other; it looked very impressive. Peter's motorbike had the front wheel slightly raised to give it that touch of class. The glass cabinet made me smile. It had a manequin of Peter standing upright, with all his gear on, leather jacket, trousers, boots and gloves. They had positioned his gloves so that it appeared that he was holding them both in his hands. The visor was down on his helmet, giving him a mystic look.

I walked over to the receptionists. 'Good morning, Sir,' they said.

'Good morning, ladies. I have two of our managers and their families arriving this morning. Could you send the two gentlemen up to my office and the ladies to the dining room in the hotel restaurant, please? If you wish to accompany them up there, please do. We are putting a new restaurant in the foyer. It will be for the general public as well as business, so you will be able to direct people to it soon. Now, what do you think of the antique cars?'

'They look very impressive, Sir.'

'I had them put there so you could be very proud of them. Thank you, ladies, have a good day.'

I saw the painters and tradesmen working at the new restaurant. Everything appeared to be going very well, so I went back up to my office and sat down.

Grumpy now owns the steam yacht, so I don't need to work on that paperwork. I opened the safe again and took out some more papers. I smiled. The safe was nearly empty. When it's empty, my job will be done. I closed the safe, went into the kitchen and made myself a cup of coffee. Before going back to my desk, I looked straight down at the construction site. It will be a self-contained city of its own, taking some of the pressure off the City of London. A city within a city. Is this where you want me to put Michelle to begin her future with her company? I asked out loud. She did well on the car park at the airport, but this is so much bigger.

A knock at the door startled me. 'Come in.'

CHAPTER 23

Five men walked into the office, followed by the receptionist, who gestured to one of the gentlemen with her hand.

'This gentleman has a meeting with Miss Smith today.' He was a large man dressed in motorcycle gear. He put his hand out to mine. The handshake was comfortable, but it let me know not to give him any trouble.

'Ronald Kolhman, Sir. I have a meeting with Michelle Smith.'

'So, you are the computer man.'

'Yes, I am.'

'I'm very pleased to meet you, Ronald. Michelle told me you're a friend of hers from university.'

Ronald laughed, 'I would say more of a playmate. She was good fun, but now she's sharp, and right down to business.'

I asked the receptionist, 'Could you please take this gentleman down two levels to meet our accountant, and make him a cup of coffee. Ronald, where is your motorbike?'

'Parked on the curb.'

'I'm an Australian, my curiosity sometimes gets the better of me, what make is it?'

'Harley-Davidson. They're the best.'

'I think, Ronald, that you had better put it in the basement garage where it will be safer.' I nodded to the receptionist. 'Could you show him the one in the foyer, please?'

'Yes, Sir, I would be delighted to do so.' They left.

I spoke with the other four gentlemen. 'Now, gentlemen, thank you for coming. Please take a seat. Do you all drink coffee?'

One man said, 'Yes, we do.'

I went into the kitchen and made four cups of coffee, put them on a tray and walked back into the office. The men were looking at the steam yacht model. 'Very impressive, isn't she?'

'Yes, she is,' one of the men replied. 'We used to have our meetings on her.'

I put the tray of coffees down on the coffee table and put my hand out to the first man. 'Hello, I am Trevor.'

He grinned at me. 'My name is Kevin Berry.' I shook hands with the other men. Their names were Terry, who was Kevin's assistant, David Reid and Geoffrey Thompson. Geoffrey was David's assistant. They all sat down and took their coffee.

'Gentlemen, I must apologise for not seeing you sooner, but I've had a few things to sort out on behalf of Peter Smith. Could you please advise me about what has been happening since Peter died?'

The two managers glanced at each other, looking annoyed. Kevin spoke first. 'It's hard to know where to start. We would try phoning Neil Gilham but could only get through to Naomi, and that was only if she wasn't in a meeting. Peter used to let us run our own race, and we sorted out our own problems. We ordered our own equipment and stores and hired who we thought was the right person for the job. Now that has all stopped, and we have to go through Marketing and Sales, which has become very frustrating. We were told that we were getting new fork-lifts, then they were cancelled, which was a big problem for us. We have put in a request for stores, but we wouldn't get what we needed. It is very hard to keep the factories running efficiently. We'd then receive some stores, and then another truck with stores would arrive. We were told not to touch those stores. The next day, another truck would turn up and take them away. We were having to sign for them arriving but not sign for them leaving.'

David spoke. 'On Friday a truck turned up, and took away one of our forklifts, saying that the lease had run out.'

'Yours the same, Kevin?'

'Yes, Trevor.'

'So, gentlemen, let's get something sorted out right here and now. Go back to the old system where you have total control of your factories. On my authority. Cancel the lease on your remaining forklifts, and lease others of your choosing, to suit your factories. Secondly, the two trucks that deliver the stores to your warehouses, do not let them leave! Use them. I will have two security officers with you on Monday morning for one week. Please don't let your staff interfere with them, let's just say, they can get a bit rough. Now are there any other problems?'

Kevin spoke again. 'Yes, there is. As you know, we make leather gear. We make everything that's made of leather: handbags, sheath cases for knives, saddles for horses, for the army, police and the military, even for the Queen's guard. We have been doing very well. Now, one of my best girls has hurt her back because I couldn't buy a new chain for the trolley, which takes the weight of the saddles. She had been lifting them by hand, and consequently damaged her back. I put in a report but got no answer, so I put in another report. My girl Penny is lying in traction in the hospital. She received a letter from Ross Uren, the lawyer, stating that she had injured her back when she was 14 years old, playing basketball, so was not covered.' He shouted out, 'She's now 51 bloody years old and one of the best workers I've got!'

I replied, 'Kevin, on Monday morning I will sort this out. Anything you have from Ross Uren, please forward to my secretary, Chris.

Disregard any instructions you have from him. He doesn't work for me or any insurance company. Send me an e-mail on Monday morning to let me know where your girl is. You said her name is Penny?'

'Yes, Penny Fletcher, we call her Henny Penny.'

'Geoffrey, do you have any problems?'

'Yes, I do. My biggest problem is that I had two women running my office. They were the best, and I never had to worry at all. Mrs Gilham rang and spoke to both of them. Next thing, they both handed in their notice and left. I couldn't do anything about it. Their retrenchment packages would have been quite large too. I don't know what she said to them, and they won't talk to me. They have been with me for a long time. Peter loved them and always told them so.'

'E-mail my secretary Monday morning with all the information you have, and their home addresses.' I slapped my hand on the desk. 'I will sort it out.'

'Another small problem, Trevor. Our assistants were both given hire cars, just a moderate car to use. Naomi Gilham cancelled them.'

'I would suggest you both pick up your assistants on Monday morning, so they can drive their cars home. This problem will also be sorted out.'

They gave me an envelope. 'Kevin said we should put down a few words on paper to assist you.'

'Thank you, gentlemen. I think we all need a drink. To the bar, gentlemen.'

As we were going up in the lift to the restaurant, I said to David. 'I know you make electrical equipment in your factory. Could you elaborate for me?'

'Yes, Trevor, we make electric motors for just about everything, AC and DC. We have government contracts for the military and the navy. We make power points, electrical cables and motors for hair dryers, electric blinds, pretty much anything that needs to be driven by an electric motor. We have plans for cars, but Bill is looking into the legal side of that before we go ahead.'

'Thank you, David, that puts me in a better picture.' The lift doors opened, and we got out. We could hear the women chattering away.

Kevin said, 'These are our wives, so we have to be on our best behaviour.'

'I know nothing, I will just agree. To the bar first, gentlemen.'

We had a very successful afternoon, and June was in her element, chatting first to this lady, and then to all of them. She was the perfect hostess. For me, that was another problem solved.

I said to June, 'I'm going to slip away for a few moments; hold the fort for me.' She nodded. I said to the gentlemen, 'Be back in a moment.' I went down to Neville's office. Ronald was sitting in front of Neville's computer, tapping on the keyboard. Michelle had another lady with her.

'Trevor, could I introduce you to Pananda, Ronald Kolhman's wife.' I felt I had met her before, but where? She had a twinkle in her eyes, which let you know she was enjoying herself. She was watching Ronald do his magic with a computer. She was dressed correctly to be a passenger on a motorbike, but she let you know she was a switched-on lady, and in complete control of herself. I knew where I stood with her.

'I'm very pleased to meet you Pananda, how is everything working out?'

'Ronald has found the problem because the computer has been tampered with, and he has to put it right. In Ronald's words, the computer is very sick, and confused!'

'That, I can't help you with. I will leave it to you. Michelle, could you please give me a lift home?'

'Yes, Trevor.'

Just then, Frank walked in. 'G'day Trevor. Michelle, my football team's winning, I've been watching them on the other computer.'

Michelle looked annoyed and put her finger to her mouth as to say, *be quiet.* I left and went back up to the restaurant. I was very pleased with how the afternoon had gone. Everybody soon went home, shaking my hand as they left. I went back down to see Michelle.

'This computer is very sick. Would you have another one to replace this one?' Ronald asked.

'I don't know what's in the company stores.'

'I will ring the storeman and ask,' Michelle answered. She went to another computer, found his phone number and called him. 'Good afternoon, Tim. I'm ringing on behalf of Trevor Evans; do you have another computer in the store that we can use?' He spoke with her for a couple of minutes, then she handed the phone to Ronald. He just said, 'No, and yes,' and looked very confused, so I put my hand out for him to give me the phone.

'It is Trevor Evans here. Is there a problem? I would be very grateful if you would come in and show Mr Kolhman what computers you have in store. I know it is Saturday, but I have a problem to solve. How long will you be? Thank you.' I hung up. 'By the time we have a coffee, Tim will be here.'

Michelle grinned at me. 'Does he know where we are? We didn't tell him.' She rang his mobile again. 'Tim, we are in the Accounts department, in Neville's office.'

Pananda made coffee, and we chatted.

Michelle said to Pananda, 'What are you doing now?'

'I've just finished a contract and I'm reading the terms for another one.'

Michelle grinned at me, then said to Pananda, 'I know of a company that will be looking for a Sales and Marketing Director. Would you be interested? You have all the qualifications they need.'

Pananda grinned at Michelle. 'You're still playing games, if it's the company I think it is. I would accept the position.'

Michelle looked at me. 'I've just found our Sales and Marketing Director.' She looked very serious and said to Pananda, 'Mrs Kolhman, we would be delighted for you to take that position. We will inform you when to start and let you know your salary and your entitlements. We just have a little problem to sort out first.' I was very impressed. What would Peter think of that.

A man walked in holding the hand of a boy about 11 years old and a girl about 14 or 15 years old. She looked very grumpy as she followed them in. I put my hand out to him. 'Thank you for coming in on your day off.' I shook his hand and said, 'I also have a daughter, and when she was fourteen, she was always saying, *I'm bored*! Now I will leave you with Ms Smith. And leave Ronald to look at the computers you have in store. I will take care of your problem.' I said to the children. 'Food, lots of lovely food.' I asked the boy, 'What's your favourite food?'

'Ice cream with white chocolate and strawberry topping,' he replied.

'Well, we can take care of that.' I asked the girl. 'What's your favourite food?'

'Honey prawns with spaghetti.'

'We can take care of that as well. We are going to the top of the building so you can see the view of London, and that is where the restaurant is. I'm going to have some honey prawns as well.' Off we went to the lift.

Michelle and Ronald went down to the store with Tim. There were three racks of computers in boxes. Ronald went down the boxes slowly, reading what was on them. Then he said to the store manager, 'Do you have any more here?'

'Yes, I have two over here, but they belong to Ross Uren.'

Michelle's voice boomed out. 'Ross Uren doesn't own anything here. He has nothing to do with this company.'

Ronald read what was on the boxes, and his eyes lit up. 'These are the latest and they are the best.'

Tim said, 'I will get the trolley.'

'I will have one, and on Monday take the other one to Mr Evans's office,' Michelle said.

Tim delivered one computer to Michelle's office. Ronald was like a little boy with a new toy, playing with the new computer. He said to Michelle, 'This is now set up. First thing in the morning, you will come here, sit down in front of this computer, and I will go to the house and transfer all the information onto this computer. It is empty and clean. I will ring you from the house and tell you what to do, and then it will be ready for Monday morning.

Now somebody said something about ice-cream!' He shut the computer down. 'Let's go see what ice-cream your children are having.'

They all left and went to the lift. When they reached the restaurant, they saw me sitting by a window with a Scotch and dry ginger looking down at the construction site. The children were happily eating away and sipping their drinks.

Ronald said, 'Where's the menu with the ice-cream?'

I handed him the menu and said to Pananda, 'This is your restaurant; this is where you eat and bring your clients. If they're from overseas, the helicopter is available, and so is the hotel.' Her eyes flitted around the restaurant and the view. 'Would you like some refreshments and coffee, Pananda? Tim, take a seat. Would you like some ice-cream? Your son seems to be enjoying his, or would you prefer something a little stronger?'

Everyone ordered, and we sat chatting for a while. Michelle told me what was happening with the computers and how we had acquired the new ones. I smiled at her. 'Michelle, on Monday morning you and Bill will be with me. From now on, you will always be with me.'

As Michelle and I drove home, she asked me, 'Where exactly do you live in Australia?'

'Jackie and I live in a lifestyle retirement village north of Melbourne in Shepparton. We used to live just outside of Melbourne, in the

Dandenong Ranges, where we had a beautiful little cottage and a bit of land. We used to enjoy feeding king parrots and kookaburras. Once, we had a pet possum, which we used to feed; she loved frozen grapes. We had three Cavalier King Charles dogs. Jackie was happy there. Time eventually caught up with us though, so we moved to Shepparton. It is much closer to our daughter, grandchildren and great-grandchildren. I really miss them. Michelle, perhaps you could fill me in. Nobody mentions your parents.'

Michelle was quiet for a moment. 'When I was 15 years old, my parents died in an avalanche in Switzerland. They were on a skiing holiday. Granny and Pop don't talk about their loss. Dad was the general manager of Pop's business. Mum was his secretary. Mum was Michael's daughter. Michael has a son as well. He travels overseas a lot, but we see him now and again. We all live with our grief in different ways.' We said nothing more on our way home.

I went to bed early but couldn't sleep. I kept thinking about the building next door. *The Trumpet.* I was totally out of my league, we were talking big money, really big money! I finally dozed off to sleep.

CHAPTER 24

When I opened my eyes, it was daylight outside, but the curtains were still closed. I thought I could hear Jackie breathing alongside me. I shook my head, idiot, Jackie's in Australia. Then who is alongside me? I slowly rolled my head over so that I could see who was there. A big pair of dark brown eyes, a long black nose, two floppy ears, golden in colour and a long body lying on its back. It was a beautiful golden retriever. I rolled over and patted it. 'What are you doing here? And where did you come from?' The dog started licking my face. Then June's voice said, 'Shirley, what are you doing in here? How many times have I told you not to get on the bed? I must apologize, Trevor. She thinks she can do whatever she likes, whenever she likes, just because she is a golden retriever. She belongs to Michael's son. He leaves her here when he's overseas.' June walked over and opened the curtains. She said sharply. 'Breakfast, Shirley.' The dog followed her.

As June was leaving, she told me to put on my dressing gown as breakfast was ready. In my mind, I could see Jackie. I looked at my watch. It said 9.50 am. I've slept in again! I didn't feel right sitting at a breakfast table in my dressing gown, but I wasn't going to argue with June. Shirley was being fed, and so was I. Chris was sitting opposite me.

'Everything go alright with Margaret's new home?'

'Yes, Trevor, she's as snug as a bug in a rug. She's very, very happy.'

Grumpy walked in and said, 'So, my son's been here. Hello Shirley, I'm not giving you back to him.' She bounced up to him, wagging her tail. Grumpy put his arms around her and gave her a big cuddle. 'When did she arrive, June?'

'Ten thirty last night. He flew in, left the dog and was gone. He said he would see you later.'

I finished my breakfast and had a shower. June had laid out a pair of grey trousers, a white shirt and a blue reefer jacket on the bed. I put them on and went into the kitchen. June was sitting there. She was wearing a white suit with royal blue trimming, blue shoes, handbag and hat, which was the shape of a feather on one side and white lace on the other. She looked as if she were going to the races.

Chris was dressed in a floral dress, beautifully coloured, with a white belt. She had matched it with white shoes and a white hat, which nearly covered one side of her head. She also looked as if she were going to the races.

Ronald grinned at me. 'Good morning, everything is fixed and back in its place, and so is the password, backed up with a lock. I'll be back on Monday morning at nine to run through everything with Neville and to install the other computer for Michelle.'

I shook his hand. 'Thank you, Ronald, that's another problem solved. Give Michelle the invoice and tell her she owes you one big favour.'

Just then, Michelle and Pananda walked into the kitchen. Michelle said, 'Good Morning all.' Shirley went down on her front legs, then ran forward, putting both her front legs on Michelle's shoulders, who put her arms around the dog and cuddled her. Shirley made a whimpering sound as she was licking Michelle's face. Michelle said to her. 'Daddy's gone walkabout again, has he?'

'You spoil that dog. It isn't your responsibility,' June said.

'Granny, every time she comes to stay, you say the same old thing and then you spoil her.'

To which June replied, 'If he didn't keep taking her back, I wouldn't get so upset.' June stamped her foot on the ground. 'Aren't we supposed to be going on a boat ride?'

She was the first one out of the door; we all followed her. The dog ran out and started running around the lawn as fast as she could, jumping up and down.

Michelle said, 'Shirley and Michael live in an apartment where the dog can't run free, so when she comes here, she just goes crazy. Mainly because she is a golden retriever.'

Shirley saw Grumpy, and she was off, running towards him. She launched herself into his arms. Grumpy held her tightly. 'My son doesn't stay, but you do, Shirley. I'm leaving my will to you. Let's go and see what I've got to eat.' They both went aboard the steam yacht.

I could see light blue smoke coming from the chimney. Grumpy has her boiler all stocked up, ready to go. As we were climbing aboard, Michelle was letting the power and stir lines go. She then climbed aboard. She nudged Grumpy away from the wheel and said, 'You are the captain; I'm the helmsman.'

The vessel gently eased away from the jetty as if she were gliding on silk. I sat down on the leather seat at the stern, just looking at the beautiful vessel, the varnish on the timber work, the beautiful panels with leather trimmings. Absolute luxury, made for a princess or a king.

As we moved up the river, with the blue smoke trailing behind us, people stopped to look at her; others were taking photos. She was part of the past when luxury was the order of the day. Grumpy put his hand out to Pananda and Ronald. 'Hi, I'm Michael, and I own this vessel. She's all mine!'

Ronald said, 'You're a very lucky man, and thank you for letting us come aboard.'

'There is a bar inside. Help yourselves,' Grumpy said. Then he brought me a Scotch and dry. I felt like a king as I watched the countryside and the big houses slide past. It was so different from Australia. England is England; you will find it nowhere else. History is there, right in front of you. Tudor buildings and Roman roads. We passed other canal boats of different shapes and sizes, but they couldn't match this old steam yacht; she is special.

Time seemed to slide past too quickly. I couldn't take it all in.

Then Michelle blew the whistle three times and started to tie her up to a jetty. At the other end of the jetty was a beautiful old English pub. It looked like a picture from an English calendar; the setting was absolutely beautiful. As we were tying up, an elderly man and lady came out of the pub. Michelle quickly ran to them. They put their arms out to Michelle, and they both cuddled each other.

Michelle said, 'Auntie Winny, I have missed you. I have been so busy since grandpa died.' Then she looked at the man. 'Uncle Ernie, you're still just as handsome as ever.'

'Michelle, stop trying to butter me up, you know you can have anything you want from me. How's that Grumpy grandfather of yours?'

'Uncle Ernie, he is the happiest man in the world. Grandpa left him the steam yacht, he now owns it, it is all his.'

'Does that mean he's going to talk to me non-stop for an hour?'

'I'm sorry to say, yes, he will, and you are going to listen to him. You helped them rebuild her.'

June's voice came from behind them. 'Hello, Ernie, it's good to see you.'

They embraced each other.

Michelle said, 'These are my friends Pananda and her husband Ronald. Ronald and I were at university together.' They all shook hands.

Ernie looked towards the steam yacht. 'Where's Grumpy? He walked off towards the vessel and climbed aboard. I was watching Grumpy tending to the boiler and wiping it down with a damp cloth. A voice boomed out. 'Where are you, old Grumpy?'

'Minding my own business Barrow boy.'

'Well, get on with it. Lunch isn't going to wait for ever.' He put his hand out to me. 'I'm Ernie, you must be Trevor. I'm very pleased to meet you. Five years ago, Smithy talked about you. I know Grumpy's in love, so we will leave him to make love to his boiler and this beautiful old lady.'

We slowly walked up to the pub. Ernie said, 'Grumpy's daughter left behind a beautiful, sharp and very intelligent granddaughter. I have two sons but consider Michelle as my daughter as well. My sons are a headache. They are identical twins and never stop arguing, but I should be grateful as they've taken over the slipway and the moorings for the canal barges and the hire business, so now we just run the pub.'

I suddenly remembered. 'Grumpy, I have some paperwork for you,' and took the envelope out of my inside pocket and gave it to him. 'I found this in the safe.'

'I've been looking for these; we need to know where to put the blocks under her keel. Thank you, Trevor.'

I stopped walking to look at the old pub. Ernie chuckled to himself. 'Yes, Trevor, she is beautiful. We don't know how old she is, but I have been told by the Reverend in the local church that it goes right back to Richard, The Lionheart. In the stonework, there is a Knights Templar Cross. I noticed that you wear a Masonic ring, so you would understand. In the scullery there is a big stone oven; my wife loves it. She sorts out the firewood so that she has bigger logs for cooking, which requires more heat, and the smaller ones for cakes, etc. She cooks on it all the time.'

We went through a low-beamed door. Luckily, I didn't hit my head as I have done in the past. I stood there looking at the big dining room. There were old English swords and shields on the walls, pictures of old buildings and old canal boats being pulled by draught horses. There were pictures of past kings and queens. Two statues of men in armour.

The tables all had beautiful green tablecloths and lovely flower arrangements in the middle of them. All the tables were beautifully set out with cutlery. The chairs were padded green velvet. Most of the tables already had people sitting at them, all very nicely dressed. I loved the big fireplace and the horse regalia that hung alongside it. With old plates on the mantelpiece. I saw Ronald sitting at a table next to the fire. He had a pint in his hand and was looking very content.

'What have you done with the women, Ronald?'

'They have gone to help prepare the meal.'

Ernie asked me, 'What would you like to drink, Trevor?'

'A Scotch and dry for me, thank you.'

'Well, sit yourself down and I'll get you one.'

'What do you think about this, Ronald?'

'It just takes your breath away, Trevor. They're changing all the pubs lately to be more fancy-dancy, to cater for the younger generation. This is wonderful.'

The four women turned up and sat down at the table.

Pananda said, 'Ronald, you've got to look at the old stove before we leave. It is so old, it's built at waist height, but it's got lots of different sized ovens to cook various foods, and you use different firewood for whatever it is you're cooking. The wood is kept underneath, and there are three spits for roast beef, pork, chickens and ducks and anything else you want to name. There is even a special place to cook your ham.'

Young waitresses, all nicely dressed in blue and frilly lace, served every table with Ambrosia Salad, along with pieces of fish, scallops, oysters, mussels, winkles that had been shelled and little pieces of crab.

Ronald chuckled. 'All of this is for me!' Pananda gave him that wifely look. When we had finished this course. Soup bowls of Lobster Bisque were served with white wine. We sat and talked, looked out of the windows at the beautiful garden and flowers. I liked the way the silver birch trees had been planted.

A waiter came up to us and advised that we were welcome to come up to the buffet and choose whatever we liked to eat and as much as we wanted.

I shook my head, why isn't Jackie here? She would have love this food. There were slices of ham on a silver tray, Beef Wellington, pork, chicken, and duck. In a silver bowl there were large prawns; another bowl had crab. Trout was laid out on a silver platter. In another section of this buffet were the vegetables, bowls of minted baby potatoes, green vegetables and cauliflower dipped in a cheese sauce, Brussel sprouts, four different types of gravy and sauces. The plate they handed to you was very large and appeared to be made of silver. Pananda said to me, 'Ronald is going to faint in a minute; he's got to make a decision.' We all filled our plates and returned to the table. There was another Scotch and dry waiting for me and red wine for the others. Then I noticed Grumpy wasn't there.

'June, where is Grumpy?'

'Trevor, you'll have to excuse him. Where he was brought up in London, he never had the opportunity to go to dinners like this, and so he feels totally out of place. He likes to sit out in the garden with the twins. He can talk to them and enjoy his meal.'

'Yes, June, I perfectly understand, this is not for everybody, but the food is.'

We eventually finished our meal, and I was content. Ronald was patting his tummy; he was quite happy. One of the young ladies came up to us and said, 'If you would like to come up to the buffet and choose your sweets.'

I stared at her for a moment. No, she isn't joking, she's serious. I slowly got up with the others and we all walked to the buffet. There were an assortment of jellies, different flavoured ice creams, fruit, strawberries, little treacle tarts, blackberry and raspberry sorbets, gooseberries, bowls of thick and thin cream, yoghurt and strawberries in Cointreau. I said to Pananda. 'I think I might faint!'

We were given another big silver plate, and they kept putting sweets onto it. I asked them to please stop, as I didn't know where I was going to put it all. Ronald looked so happy. We returned to our table, and there was another Scotch and dry waiting for me. I thoroughly enjoyed the sweets, but I couldn't eat it all. On top of all of that, another silver tray with glasses of liqueur turned up, and a platter of cheese and another one of cakes. If ever I could say I was done for, then this was it.

June smiled at me. 'I was going to warn you to start off slow, but I forgot.'

Just then, the two twins stood behind Michelle. 'We would like to talk to you Michelle, we have been suffering far too long.' They both talked perfectly together, as one; we were all amused. 'When we last met, we talked about which of us you were going to marry. Could you let us know which of us it is?'

Michelle glanced over at me and winked, then she looked down at the table as though she was having trouble. She looked up at the two boys with so much compassion and sorrow on her face. 'I've had trouble trying to sort out which one of you would be best for me and how I could make you happy. I know I can't marry one of you, though, as the other will be totally shattered. I've come to a very sad decision, and it has been very hard as you are both absolutely wonderful, but with a very heavy heart, I must say no to both of you.' Michelle looked like a pleading puppy; it was all I could do to stop laughing.

The twins looked at each other with sadness and together, they both said, 'We must go back to the drawing board and find another set of twins.' Then they both turned at the same time and walked off to the slipway.

I could see Michael sitting at a table outside feeding the dog with treats, which looked rather large to me; in fact, they looked like slices of ham. I looked at Chris. She looked very content and happy, enjoying her liqueur. I saw Win and Ernie walking up to the table where Michael was and sit down. I could see them talking to him. He nodded. They got up, and I presume that they went back to the kitchen.

I asked Michelle, 'Where's the love of your life?'

She smiled; his football team won on Saturday, so he's with his friends celebrating. I didn't stand in his way. I've got big plans for him, and I've thoroughly enjoyed today, especially watching the others relaxing.'

Time had caught up with us again, and it was time to leave. We said our goodbyes and thank you's for a wonderful day.

On the return trip, I sat in the stern with June, Chris and Michelle.

Grumpy walked up to Michelle and said to her. 'I'm the captain; you're the helmsman. To the helm, girl!'

Michelle got up and saluted Grumpy. 'Yes sir,' and she went to the wheel. Ernie let the line go, and Michelle used the stern line to swing her bow out into the river, then waved goodbye. We were on our way home.

I looked at Pananda. She was sitting there looking very content. She had a beautiful smile on her face. Ronald was sitting alongside her, but he looked like he had dozed off to sleep. He also had a contented grin on his face. What a good day.

Michelle eased up the mooring, and we were home from a day of pure luxury.

CHAPTER 25

On Monday morning, Michelle and I landed on the roof in the helicopter. 'Michelle, could you ask Frank to come up to my office with you? Chris, could you raise an order for two lease cars for both factories, a vehicle you could take a whole family in. Please also organise the insurance for the two assistant managers of the factories and put their wives' names on that as well, but nobody else.'

Chris asked, 'Any particular colour?'

'White, Chris, it stands out in the dark. Could you give me Freddy's telephone number, please?'

I rang Freddie. 'Good morning, Freddie, hope it's not too early.'

'It's always too early!' he replied.

'Freddie, I need two security officers. One at each of the factories for one week. The manager will tell your man what he wants.'

Freddie asked me for the addresses.

'Good question, Freddie.' I handed the phone to Chris, who gave him the addresses.

Michelle and Frank walked into the office. 'Good morning, Frank.'

'Good morning, Trevor.'

'Frank, one of the women who works in the leather factory has injured her back, and we are going to see her this morning. Her name is

Penny; they call her Henny Penny. Could you get her particulars, please? Then we are going to see the two ladies who were dismissed from the electrical factory. Could you get their addresses, please?'

'Trevor, you have an appointment with the City Fathers concerning the site next door,' Chris said.

'Chris, could you let Bill know? What time is the meeting?'

'10.30 am. Your friend from Dubai will be there as well.' Then Chris said, 'On Wednesday morning at 10.30 you have a meeting with a sergeant from the police force, a Tiny Harrison and a detective inspector from the fraud squad, a Chris O'Hara.' I raised my eyebrows.

Michelle said to me, 'This afternoon I would like to go through my grandfather's notes concerning the site next door, so if you could drop me back home after we've seen the ladies, that would be great.'

I went to the safe and took some money out, closed the safe and asked Chris for three envelopes. I put some money in each of them and put them in my inside jacket pocket.

'Are you ready, Frank?' He was still sitting at the computer, jotting notes down on a piece of paper.

Michelle said to Chris, 'There's a new computer coming up to the office; the man you met yesterday at lunch, Ronald, will be here to install it. I would prefer it not to be on Trevor's desk. It would look out of place. Could you find another desk, please?'

Chris smiled. 'Yes, I know where there's another desk that will suit this office.'

'Thank you, Chris.'

Michelle and Frank stood behind me in the lift, but I could see their reflection in the panelling. Young love! I find it very amusing when lovers don't think anybody is watching. We got out of the lift and went to Frank's car. 'Where are we going, Frank?'

'To Croydon hospital, Trevor.'

'I was born at Croydon Hospital 81 years ago on the 19th of September. I would imagine it's changed a lot since then.'

Frank dropped us off at the front door, then went and parked the car. We waited for him, and then we all went into the hospital together. Frank went to reception and spoke to a young lady who then spoke to another lady, who asked us to follow her. She ushered us into an office. The manager behind the desk stood up.

Frank introduced himself. 'I'm Frank Mattea. I phoned you this morning to make an appointment. My colleagues here are Penny Jones's employers, and I'm their lawyer.' We all shook hands and introduced ourselves. Frank spoke again. 'We are here to see that Ms Jones gets the best treatment by the best doctors; we will take full responsibility for her injury. So could you please inform us of her injuries and what we need to do to give her the very best care?'

The gentleman pushed some buttons on his computer and said, 'It has been very confusing as to who would take responsibility. We have had emails from a lawyer, Ross Uren, stating it was from a previous injury.'

Frank said to him, 'Ross Uren does not work for this company and has nothing to do with this situation. Her work colleagues were with her when the situation happened. I have been informed that she has a swollen disc, and that it needs surgery to repair it.'

'Now we know who is taking responsibility, we can do something. I would suggest that we hand it over to Mr Robert Carey; he is the best there is to treat this.'

'If you could draw up the paperwork, we will sign it now,' Frank said.

The manager said, 'If you would like to go up and see her, I will bring the paperwork up to you. Her next of kin is involved, and they are with her now. If you go to the fourth floor, turn to the right, take the first left; she is in that ward.'

'Thank you.'

As we were going up in the lift, I wondered to myself, whereabouts was I born in this hospital?

We walked into the ward. Frank asked the nurse where Penny was, and she ushered us to a cubicle. There was a man standing there, about fifty years of age, carrying a bit of weight, about my height, with grey hair. He had a young woman with him. She had blonde hair, which was nicely groomed over her shoulders. She was very attractive and smartly dressed.

I said, 'Good morning. I am Trevor Evans. This is Michelle and Frank, who is our company lawyer. First, I must apologise to you, Penny, for the runaround the company has given you.'

'Thank you.'

'Any correspondence you might have received from the company, please disregard it. We are here to put things right.' I turned to the man. 'I presume you are her husband, and I put my hand out.'

He frowned at me but shook my hand.

'Now Penny, you will have the best surgeon we can get. They have told us that you have a damaged disc, and that it needs to be repaired. Your wages since the accident will be back-paid to you, and you will be paid for the whole time you are off work. When your doctor says you can return to work, we will find you work that is easier for you.'

I put my hand into my inside pocket and took out one envelope. 'This is to cover any expenses you might have incurred to date.' I gave her the envelope. 'Is your television working?'

'No, it isn't; we have to pay for it.'

Frank said to her, 'Consider it done. Is there anything else we can help you with?'

I could see the tears in her eyes. I reached out and held her hand. 'We are so sorry. Your colleagues in the factory tell us you are the best, and you have given Peter Smith many years of excellent service. We will stand by you, and yes, I know what it's like to be in traction. Does this bed go up and down electrically?'

'Yes, it does.'

I put my hand out again to her husband. 'If there are any problems, please ring Frank here at head office, and he will sort things out.' The manager brought us the papers, which we signed. 'Now we'll leave you to your privacy.'

Back in Frank's car, I said, 'I know exactly what she's going through. I lay in traction for many weeks. You can't turn over, and you have to lie flat on your back, not at all comfortable.'

Fifteen minutes later, we were pulling up outside a house. I was very impressed; it was my type of house. Old English. We walked up to the front door. Frank pressed the doorbell. A lady in her forties, with blonde hair, about five foot six, wearing jeans and a blouse with colourful flowers on it, opened the door. Another lady stood behind her. She appeared to be in her forties as well. She had brown hair and was also wearing jeans with a Manchester T-shirt. We were ushered into a neatly furnished lounge room.

'I believe you are Jennifer, and you are Isabel?' Michelle said. 'I am Michelle Smith, Peter Smith's granddaughter, and this is Trevor Evans and Frank, whom I believe you've met before?'

'Yes, we have.'

Michelle continued, 'We would like to apologise to both of you for what has happened. My grandfather, Peter Smith, would have been horrified at how you have been treated. He considered you both the best he had and highly valued you both. We would be most grateful if you would consider returning to work this coming Tuesday. You will be reimbursed financially and have an increase in your salary.'

'Would we still be working under Ross Uren and Naomi Gilham?' Jennifer asked.

'No, you only answer to the manager of the factory. Ross Uren does not work for this company and has nothing to do with it. In the future, Naomi Gilham will be leaving.'

They looked at each other. 'Then we will return on Tuesday.'

Michelle smiled at them. 'We are so grateful to you both. Now, just for our record, what did Naomi Gilham say to you?'

'She said that she had found errors in our paperwork. We tried to contact the accounts department but were put through to Naomi Gilham. We told her what we had found, and she said we were totally incompetent and were interfering with company policy and that we should just do our job and shut up. She said if we didn't like it, we could leave. Then she hung up. On the spur of the moment, we handed in our notice. We have regretted it. All the time we were at the company, it was very good to us. When Frank rang us and asked to have a meeting, we were very worried.'

I put my hand in my inside pocket and took out two envelopes. 'Ladies, please accept these. They don't put things right, but please accept them as out-of-pocket expenses.'

I put my hand out and shook their hands. We chatted for a while, then we left them saying, thank you. On our way back, we dropped Michelle off at the house and went back to the office. I liked the desk that Chris had found for the computer; it fitted in perfectly with the office. It always puzzled me; Ross Uren couldn't have been the only one involved in making this a public company. 'Chris, do you know how this fancy computer works?'

She frowned at me. 'No, I don't know Trevor. I only understand my computer, so you'll have to speak with Bill.'

I picked up my phone and pressed Bill's button. He answered. 'Yes, Trevor, how can I help you?'

'Hi Bill, do you have a moment to come up to my office, please?'

'On the way, Trevor.'

I shouted out, 'Two coffees, Fussy.'

She shouted back. 'Would you like some chocolate biscuits too?'

Chris's voice boomed out. 'They are my chocolate biscuits.'

'They were your biscuits; now they're ours.'

She brought them in to me. I thanked her.

Bill walked in the door. 'Good afternoon, Bill.'

'G'day to you, Trevor, and you too, Madam.' Chris twinkled her fingers in the air but said nothing.

'Bill, I want to get something straight in my mind, and perhaps this computer will give me the answers. Ross Uren couldn't have been trying to make this a public company on his own. There must have been others involved, and I would like to know who they are.'

'Trevor, I already know. One is Cedric Wallass; he's a high-flying lawyer. He has degrees as long as your arm but is not the sort of man you would want to tangle with. Another gentleman who is a judge and who, for political reasons, I'm not able to give you his name. Another is Simon Games, a lawyer, and Freddie Mitchell. Freddie and I were at university together. He told me in confidence that they all wanted to become shareholders. I couldn't do anything about it. I was the company lawyer, and that was where my jurisdiction ended. Now, the only other person who knows what I do is Chris. Trevor, in a manner of speaking, I went around the back door and spoke to a man high up in government circles. The judge was dismissed on the grounds of a conflict of interest. After that, the gentleman in question stepped in, and the problem was sorted out. Now you are here.'

Bill looked at Chris. She was concentrating on her computer. He slowly got out of his chair and crept over behind Chris, took a handful of the chocolate biscuits and sat back in his chair. He then enjoyed his coffee and chocolate biscuits. He looked at my computer, got up out of his chair and came and stood looking closer at the new computer. 'Trevor, this is the latest computer, the Ferrari sports car of computers.'

'Would you like it, Bill?'

'Yes, I would.'

'Bill, you are the lawyer for a very large organisation; if you want one, order it. I know it would be in the company's best interest, looking into the future and politics, to order two. One for you and one for Frank.'

'Trevor, I think we're both playing the same game concerning Michelle.' We both grinned at each other. Chris turned around, looking at both of us and grinned as well.

'Trevor, if you would excuse me, I have a bit of paperwork to finish.' As he got to the door, he put his hand up in the air and twinkled his fingers. 'Chris, bye darling,' and he left.

'How do I say thank you to the man, Chris?'

'You just did, Trevor. You gave him a new toy to play with; like all men, he is just a little boy. I agree with you both. If Michelle had ordered the computer for Frank, it would have looked like favouritism.'

I looked at my watch, 4.30pm. Where's the day gone? 'Chris, I'm heading home. I just want to sit quietly somewhere and think.'

'Yes, Trevor, it will be a big day tomorrow.'

The helicopter landed on the lawn. I got out and walked to one side as it took off again.

Shirley was there to greet me. I gave her plenty of attention and said hello to June. She smiled at me. 'I'm going down to the boat to sit and think and sort things out in my mind.'

June said. 'Could you give Grumpy this shovel? He fed the dog yesterday, so now he can clean the poos up!'

I walked down to the boat, shovel in one hand, bottle of scotch in the other.

CHAPTER 26

I opened my eyes to the sound of June opening the curtains. 'Wake up, Trevor, you've got a big day ahead. I have laid out a business suit for you, and I believe an appropriate tie. Come on, Shirley, wake up, and I will feed you.' Shirley shot off the bed and was in the kitchen before June.

I felt quite smart in this suit; it certainly was well tailored. I went and sat at the breakfast table. I looked at Michelle and wondered, is this the day she will be ready?

'How are you this morning Michelle?'

'A little nervous, Trevor.'

'I believe we should keep it strictly business, Michelle.'

'I've been through my grandfather's files, and he has given me all the information I need, in a manner of speaking. He said to keep it strictly business too. But who can I trust and who can't I? Am I ready?'

'Are you coming into the office with me in the helicopter?'

'Yes, Trevor.'

When we arrived at our London office, Bill was waiting for us. We said our good mornings, and Michelle walked over to her computer and patted it with so much affection, saying, 'This will take me into the future.'

A voice from the kitchen said, 'Three coffees?'

'Yes, please,' I said.

Fussy came out of the kitchen with one coffee on a plate and a chocolate biscuit. She gave it to Bill and then went back into the kitchen and brought the other coffees out.

I said, 'There's no favouritism in my office, is there, Bill?' Bill put his hand into his inside pocket and took out two envelopes. 'Michelle, these are the documents you asked me to prepare.' He gave her one of the envelopes. She smiled at him, raising her eyelids, then he gave her the second envelope.

'On Friday morning at 11, there will be a gentleman to watch you land and take off from the top of this building in the helicopter. This is the last part of your ticket to officially fly one. I know you've done it at the airport, but he wants you to do it off this building.' She wasn't smiling and looked very serious. She drank her coffee quickly.

I went to the safe and took out the piece of paper that Peter had sketched a tower on and put the figure underneath. Except for some money, the safe was now empty. Is that telling me something?

'Your car is waiting down in the foyer,' Chris said. Bill and Michelle picked up their briefcases, and we all went down to the foyer, where a government car was waiting for us. After a short drive, we pulled up outside an impressive-looking building.

'This is the back of #10 Downing Street,' Bill said.

We got out of the car and were ushered into the building and taken to a conference room. The first man was Ali, from Dubai, but he was dressed in a suit, not a Kandura. I nodded to him; he nodded back. His colleague was also dressed in a nice suit. Another gentleman with a nicely trimmed beard came in with a walking stick, which sported a beautiful silver handle. I stood there staring at him for a moment. Something about him puzzled me, but what? Another three gentlemen and a lady came into the room. The lady sat down at the table and put a laptop computer in front of her, all ready to record the conversation. The gentleman with the neatly trimmed grey beard spoke first.

'Good morning, ladies and gentlemen. Thank you for coming today. I am Sir John Moore; the gentleman on my right is Sir Chadwick Wallace. The gentleman on my left,' he gestured with his left hand, 'is Sir Colin Hare. Please be seated, ladies and gentlemen.'

I looked at Sir Chadwick Wallace. I felt angry. So, this was the man who wanted to play games with Peter Smith's company.

Sir Chadwick stood up and started to talk. 'Ladies and gentlemen, we are here to discuss the future of one block of land that is very important to the people of London and its government. As you are aware, we would like to purchase that block of land, but in the interests of the City of London, it must be at the right price.'

I couldn't contain myself. I stood up and said, 'With due respect to you, Sir John, I feel I must interrupt this gentleman. He has been involved in trying to take over my company for his own interest. If he continues, we will leave. I will suggest to him to sit down and be silent.'

He sat down, looking very angry. Sir John raised his eyebrows and had a slight grin on his face. I looked at Michelle, and she stood up.

'Sir John, I am Michelle Smith, granddaughter of Peter Smith. I have all the information concerning this business arrangement. I repeat, business arrangement. Just before my grandfather died, a contract was drawn up between you and him, the price was also negotiated. It is unfortunate that he died but we will stand by his wishes and this contract. He also informed me that I could trust you one hundred percent.'

Sir John stared at her seriously. Had Michelle checkmated him? Then he burst out laughing. 'You certainly are Peter Smith's granddaughter; we will honour that contract.'

He looked at the gentleman on his left.

Sir Colin said, 'Yes.'

Sir John said, 'I need to confer with my immediate superiors first, but we will meet back here tomorrow at 4 pm.'

Just then, Sir Chadwick stood up and said, 'I have a very busy day tomorrow!'

To which Sir John replied, 'This has been going on for five years, we don't particularly need you tomorrow. Thank you, ladies and gentlemen, our business is now finished for today. There are refreshments waiting for you.'

The very elderly gentleman walked over to us and put his hand out to me. 'I am Edward Gilham, and yes, I am his father. Neil is my son. I have a big problem. I am 90 years old. Peter Smith and I were training him to take my place. I am the head of an international banking system. I cannot let Neil take command while he is married to Naomi. She makes it far too dangerous. If my son divorces her, it will create too many problems. I have a feeling, Trevor, that you will find the answer. Now, Michelle, in your contract with the government, you don't pay tax on the three payments you will receive over three years.'

Michelle said, 'That is correct.'

'Your grandfather left you quite a bit of money in trust. At our bank, we loan that money out with interest to make money. The government is going to borrow that money for your land from us. If we loan the first payment from your money to the government, you will get a higher rate of interest, and the government doesn't need to know it's your money. It just comes out of our bank loan account. Are you interested?'

Michelle smiled. 'Yes, I am. If you could talk to Bill here, he will do all the paperwork.'

I went over to Ali and his companion. 'Good day to you both.'

Ali put his hand on his heart and bowed his head.

'Ali, I have a suggestion for you that may work in your interest.' I talked to him discreetly about my plan; he nodded. I continued talking, and he agreed with what I said.

Ali smiled. 'Yes, Trevor, consider it done. Now, Trevor, could I ask you to do something for me? My colleague and I would like to go to an English nightclub.'

'When, Ali?'

'Would tonight be okay?'

'Yes, I can arrange that. Are you staying at my hotel?'

'Yes, we are.'

'Good, then at 7 pm I will have a car waiting for you.' Discreetly, I got in touch with Freddy, and he arranged everything for me. I went back to Michelle. 'You, Frank and I are going out on the town tonight with Ali and his companion. Would you like to come too, Bill?'

'No thank you, Trevor, I have the children tonight, but thank you for asking.'

We mingled with the others, drinking coffee and tea. Everything was kept very polite, and I must admit, I did very much enjoy the cucumber sandwiches without crusts.

Eventually, we all left. I was so proud of Michelle; she handled everything perfectly. It was over and done with quickly—no politics—just straight business. But what did Neil's father mean by *I would sort out the problem for them.* I had enjoyed my conversation with Ali; it could be one of the last of my problems solved.

I said to Michelle, 'Freddy has booked a car to pick us up at 7 pm. Do you want to go home to change first?'

'Yes, Trevor, if I could. A business suit doesn't quite fit in at nightclubs. We also have a big day tomorrow with two meetings, and we need to be sharp.'

'Yes, Michelle, we are playing with the big boys and girls here.'

CHAPTER 27

When we got home, June had just taken fresh mince pies out of the oven. They went down nicely with coffee. When Michelle walked into the kitchen, I raised my eyebrows and whistled. 'You look stunning, Michelle.'

'She scrubs up well, doesn't she?' June said.

Grumpy walked in the door; he must have smelt the mince pies. He stopped and stared at Michelle. His face went very serious, and you could see the tears in his eyes, and he started to sob. 'You look just like your mum; you could be her double.' He walked over to her and put his arms around his granddaughter. June had her apron up to her face to hide her tears. I couldn't stop my tears. The dog just looked confused; she didn't know what was going on and didn't know who to go to. It was a magical moment not to be forgotten.

'June, do you have any mince pies left for our pilot?'

Michelle and I left to join the helicopter, and we gave Joe, the pilot, two of the mince pies. We soon landed back at the office building. I could see Michelle concentrating on the pilot, and on how he was land-ing the helicopter on the building, and on how he spoke to the office in charge of manning the landing pad.

We went to the lifts and down to the basement, where a stretch limousine was waiting for us. Nobody would have seen us. The car took us to Freddy's nightclub. He was there to meet us, and I introduced him to everybody. Freddy said, 'In my nightclub you are not Ali, you are Alan.' He looked at Ali's companion. 'And you are his bodyguard.' He nodded. 'You are Dick in my club. Follow me.' He led us to a table discreetly located at the rear of the club, but we could see everything going on. People were coming in and sitting down at their tables. There were three bars situated around the room and a big dancing area in the middle. There was a small glass room on one side. Freddy said to Alan, 'What happens in my nightclub, stays in my nightclub. Any trouble and I will sort it out.' Freddy clicked his fingers, and two waitresses turned up. They certainly had nice legs. They took our drink orders. 'Any time you're in England and you want to escape for a while, my club is open to you. I will provide the transport,' Freddy said to Alan. He put his left hand up to his heart, bowed slightly, touched his forehead with his left hand and stepped back. Alan did the same.

The music started, and it was loud, certainly not my type of music. Michelle and Frank got up and went to the dance floor and disappeared into the crowd. I couldn't make out what they were doing; it was just one mass of people jumping up and down, left and right, and whirling around. I took a couple of mouthfuls of my drink, but they didn't ease the confusion.

Freddy came forward with two young ladies. 'Alan, these are your companions for the night. Enjoy yourselves.' The two young ladies led Alan and Dick to the dance floor.

'Freddy, why do you call him Dick?'

'Because he is a cop, a dickhead!'

I shook my head. 'Freddy, I might have found a way to protect Naomi. I have spoken to Alan, and he may have the answer.'

'I'm just playing the game, Trevor; I have faith in you. Now I've gotta run this club and, as you said, play the game.'

He was off. I sat there sipping my drink and asking myself, what am I doing here? It certainly wasn't my world. I noticed a blonde lady standing next to the glass room and a DJ standing behind the desk with all the instruments. That is Sue Williams! I got up and walked up behind Sue, who was dancing back and forwards on her feet. 'Excuse me, young lady, what do you call that dance?'

She spun around and looked straight into my face. 'Trevor, what are you doing here?' She threw her arms around my neck.

'I'm just checking up on you, my daughter.'

'How did you get here, Trevor?'

'It's a very long story; can I buy you a drink, Sue?'

'Yes, you can.' She opened the door to the glass room. The DJ had earmuffs on. He turned around to look at Sue. He looked totally surprised. I put my hand up and made a circle with my thumb and finger and held it up in the air to him. He put his thumb up in the air and shook it at me. I pointed to Sue and myself and gestured that we were going for a drink. We went back to our table.

'What are you doing in England, Sue?'

'My friend, the DJ, was offered a contract as a DJ by a British organisation, to do various nightclubs throughout England. I wasn't going to miss out, so I joined him.'

Just then, Alan came back with his lady friend. They sat down, and I introduced them to Sue. I explained to him how I had met her and about our relationship.

Sue said, 'I'm running out of money very quickly. I've got to find a job.'

Alan looked at her seriously. 'May I call you Susanne?'

'Yes.'

'You have been well educated, and you are what they call *streetwise*.'

'Yes, she is,' I said.

'And you will vouch for her, Trevor?'

'Yes, I will.'

'Well, I'm looking for somebody like you. I'm a Prince in Dubai and very much involved in business. Women in Dubai have got to change from the past into the future if they want to travel with us. This is what we want, but we want them to understand the real world, not the history, not the politics, but how people live and survive. We must put our investments into the future; the world is shrinking rapidly. We must prepare our people for these changes. So, we need somebody like you for when our wives come with us. We need someone to show them England, the real England, and to make them streetwise. We can give them the best education, but there are some things we cannot give them, but I feel you can. We would pay you £2000 per week, and we will pay for your accommodation and all your expenses. You will stay at Trevor's hotel. There will be some weeks we will not be here, but I'm sure you will work in our interests. You are the right age. You've had your successes, and you've had your falls. You have the knowledge; are you interested?'

Sue didn't hesitate. 'Yes, I am. Can my partner stay with me?'

'Yes, but he must be discreet. You will work through Trevor's company. They have all the expertise you need.'

Freddy walked up behind me. He looked at Sue. 'Trevor, you're a fast worker.'

'Freddy, I never miss a trick. She's a good looker, isn't she?'

He smiled at me.

'Freddy, Sue is like a daughter to me; we go back a long way.'

'Well, Trevor, you've got good taste.' He walked off to do his rounds.

Alan said, 'I think I've done enough for one day, so as you would say. Home James.'

CHAPTER 28

I was so pleased to put my head on the pillow and close my eyes. There was movement on the bed, and I knew it was Shirley. It was very comforting to know that I wasn't alone.

I awoke in the morning. Daylight was just starting to creep around the curtain. Somebody had covered Shirley up with a small blanket. She looked at me with one eye; the other was still closed. 'Is it too early for you, Shirley?' She closed both her eyes. 'Yes, Shirley, it's too early, but I have a big day and I must be prepared.'

I went and had my shower. I stood there under the hot water a little longer. Was I ready for this day? No, I am playing a game, bluffing my way through. I got dressed and walked back into the bedroom. The bed was made; Shirley had gone. I looked out of the window, and what I saw took my breath away. There had been a light sprinkle of snow during the night, and it made the garden look absolutely beautiful. This was England, warm one day, cold the next, with a sprinkle of snow. That's why June had covered Shirley with a blanket.

I walked into the kitchen. Shirley was busy eating her breakfast. Michelle looked up from hers and said, 'G'day mate, how are you going?'

I replied, 'Absolutely marvellous. Good morning, June.' She turned slightly from what she was doing and noticed me. 'How long will the snow last, June?'

'It will be gone by 11 am. It is only a cold front from Russia; they don't want it, so they send it to us.'

Michelle looked at me with a puzzled expression. 'Trevor, why did Freddy call Ali's friend ****Dick?'

'Michelle, I'd better not repeat it, but he doesn't like authority and he has his own personal joke.'

Michelle grinned and nodded. I had just finished my breakfast when I heard the helicopter land. 'Ready, Michelle?'

June handed me a small paper bag. 'This is for Joe.' But Michelle took it before I could.

'While you are eating your egg and bacon sandwich, I will fly the helicopter.' Michelle said to Joe.

Joe looked at me with a surprised look.

'Joe, she owns the helicopter, and she has her licence. I can't step in and help you; our hands are in our laps.'

He made the sign of the cross and put his hands together, looking up. Before I could blink, he was eating his egg and bacon sandwich, and we were up in the air. I looked at the countryside below us with that sprinkle of snow. It was such a majestic picture that would forever stay in my mind.

'You had better land this, Joe,' Michelle said. 'I'm not doing my final exam until Friday morning. Also, could you please arrange for a two-seater helicopter for 4 pm on Friday? We will be gone for the long weekend.'

She looked at me. 'Frank and I have to sort things out for our future, so we are going to escape for the long weekend.'

'Well, Michelle, that disappoints me. I thought you would take me too.'

'I would love to, Trevor, but I've got bigger plans for somebody.' She spoke softly with tenderness. 'I'm so sorry Trevor, not this time.'

'Michelle, now I know how Shirley feels when she's rejected.' I winked at her.

She then concentrated on what Joe was doing to land the helicopter and how he spoke to the control tower for permission to land.

We had a beautiful, soft landing. Joe asked Michelle, 'Do you have any questions?'

'Yes, I do. Do you always land the helicopter in the same direction?'

'We can't turn the helicopter around to face the other way because the tie-downs are situated to suit the helicopter, and you need to keep an eye on the windsock, to tell you which way the wind is blowing and watch your instruments.' He pointed to them on the dial. 'If I land this way, you don't have to walk around the helicopter; you can walk straight out to the left. It's all occupation, health and safety. Mention those words to the instructor.'

'Thank you, Joe. Just order a simple helicopter; the less complicated, the better.'

'I know that you already know this, but shut down your helicopter before your passengers disembark. On this particular building, I like the tie-downs to be on the helicopter as soon as we land as the winds are very unpredictable.'

Michelle nodded, and I patted him on the shoulder. Michelle and I walked into the office. Chris was already there. 'How come you got into the office so quickly, Chris?'

'I came in earlier to catch up on some work.'

'Well, Chris, that answers that. I was wondering why you weren't at breakfast.'

Just then, Bill and Frank walked into the office. They both said at the same time, 'How are you going, mate?'

I replied, 'Will you two kangaroos stop chattering like two galahs and sit down. Fussy, are you there in the kitchen?'

'Yes, I am, and I'm bringing your coffees out now. Some people are so impatient!'

'Fussy, do you have any more chocolate biscuits? Bill likes them.'

'No, I don't, but Chris has some nice chocolate doughnuts!' Chris put her hands up in the air in frustration.

I said, 'We are just playing games with time. We have another meeting at 4 pm, so the car will be here at 3.30 pm. I presume you're all ready.'

Michelle answered, 'Yes, Trevor, we are. Fussy, you provided chocolate doughnuts, so will you come with us as a witness when we sign the documents?'

Bill looked at Chris and started laughing and put his hands in the air.

Chris said, 'Could you look at this e-mail from Naomi? It says, Where has the desk gone from my foyer?' She had replied, *Ask Bill, our lawyer*.

Everybody finished their coffee with grins on their faces. We all went to the conference room. I stood looking out of the window with my hands behind my back, going through my thoughts to prepare for the meeting.

There was a knock at the door. I turned around to see Neil Gilham ushering in a young lady, Naomi, and five gentlemen into the room. He showed them to their seats, but two of the gentlemen kept standing up, against the door. They were wearing nice suits, their hair was neatly groomed, they both had moustaches, and they had Police ties on with Police badges on their lapels. They looked very professional.

One gentleman walked with a slight limp. His hair was snow white, short and well groomed. He was a big man. He moved his chair to one side and moved to another chair, which was higher, and then he sat down. I shrugged my shoulders and thought, well he's a big man he would be more comfortable in a higher chair. Another man sat down next to him. He wasn't quite as tall but was a no-nonsense man, who would be straight to the point. He was a little bit bald on top and wore dark-rimmed glasses. I noticed he was wearing a Masonic ring; it looked very impressive. Then I noticed that the first man was also wearing a Masonic ring. They both wore Police ties.

The third man made me feel very angry. How would I describe him? About 5 feet 4 inches tall, wearing a silk suit and silk tie, his hair was combed back. Next to him sat the Barbie doll, Naomi Gilham. I must admit she looked good. The young lady sat two chairs away from Naomi. She put her laptop computer on the conference table and was all ready to record the events. Neil Gilham sat on our side of the conference table.

Bill stood up. 'Ladies and gentlemen, I am the lawyer for this company. Gentlemen, if you would please introduce yourselves.'

The first man nodded. 'I am known as Tiny Harrison. I'm a Sergeant in the Police Force.'

The next man nodded. 'I am Chris O'Hara. I'm a Chief Detective Inspector in the Police Fraud Squad.'

Bill then said in a commanding voice. 'Now we all know you two, don't we?'

Tiny Harrison stood up and put a file in front of him. The names on the front of it were NAOMI GILHAM and ROSS UREN.

'Reading through some of this paperwork previously, it had puzzled me, so I made some inquiries. Mr Uren was registered as a lawyer, and before that, he was a barrister. Using that position, he gave himself the title of International Lawyer. He works very close to the fine line. Naomi Gilham was very interesting, and the more I delved into this, the more fascinating it became. Who was she before she married Neil Gilham?' I looked at Ross and Naomi. They didn't look too happy, and they were fidgeting in their seats. I looked at Sergeant Harrison, who continued informing me.

'I couldn't find a marriage certificate in England, but I was told they were married overseas on a tropical island. Interestingly, no marriage certificate was issued on that island, and if it was a marriage, it was a scam. Further research found out that she is actually married to Ross Uren.' This information was said out loud; the entire room was a witness.

Neil Gilham's chair went flying backwards as he stood up. The two policemen were at the door. They were ready for this and were standing next to Neil. One of the policemen said, 'We will escort you from the room for a while and let you cool down.' We could all feel Neil's anger and frustration. The look he gave Naomi was that of a man who was going to lose control of himself. The two policemen ushered him out of the door and closed it behind them.

Sergeant Harrison continued, 'I spoke to your previous employer, and he told me the full story. I am not a lawyer, so I can't say this in a court, but here I can. Naomi, I was informed by your previous employer that you have been groomed by this man, Ross Uren, your so-called husband. With him, you have committed a crime or crimes, for which I should charge you however, I will hand you over to my colleague, Chris O'Hara.'

Sgt Harrison sat down. Chris O'Hara stood up and took a moment to compose himself. 'Mr Uren, every time I meet a man like you, who uses the law to further his own wicked way of life, it disgusts me. I did my research on you. You call yourself an international lawyer. We checked with all your overseas associates and discovered that all of your overseas business addresses are empty shops, or empty blocks of land. The news-agency from which you have magazines sent to England through the back door and distribute to your customers are so inappropriate. Can we charge you for that? No, because you have been very discreet in the way you've done it. The magazines disgusted my colleagues greatly, so we got a Court Order to raid your apartment. You have been very clever, haven't you? We found boxes of files in a secret room. Dirty information about anybody who has ever been associated with you, including barristers, judges, lawyers, politicians and others, and even businessmen you tried to manipulate by using this company and using your wife. You've been trying to turn this company into a public company, blocking Peter Smith's wishes in his will. You have used the resources of his company to create your own business by using two of his warehouses and doing inappropriate business transactions, bringing labour in from overseas illegally and creating sweatshops. You are a problem for the British government and an embarrassment to the legal profession. If we let this go further, it would cost money and time for the public while awaiting prosecution. Both of you would find yourselves in gaol waiting for it to come up in court. Mr Evans, I believe, has the solution to satisfy the British government and his company.'

I stood up. 'Could you ask Mr Gilham to come back in, please?' The police officers brought a more subdued Mr Gilham in and sat him down.

I began to speak. 'Naomi, Freddie said to me that you are one of his girls and I was to look after you and I agreed to his request.' I pointed to my Masonic ring. 'Your contract with this company stands for another five years. I am going to sell that contract to my colleagues in Dubai because you are very good at your job and they can use your expertise. Freddie will hold on to your passport so it will be safe, and you will use a photocopy. Your lifestyle will stay the same in Dubai as it is in England.'

'Mr Uren, there are now people in England who will want to cut your throat. So, I'll give you the easy way out. You will go with your wife to Dubai; they can use your knowledge as well.'

'When?' Ross Uren asked.

I enjoyed this. 'Now!'

'What do you mean now?'

'There is a private plane waiting for you now. Naomi, your belongings will be sent to you in Dubai.'

The two police officers stepped forward and handcuffed them both, and they were ushered through the door, down to a waiting police car.

Bill stood up. 'Gentlemen, I believe that has been settled cleanly and should stop any politics or gossip. None of this information will leave this office. Mr Harrison, do you have a copy of the Uren's marriage certificate?'

'Yes, I do.'

'Could you please give one to Mr Gilham?'

Sergeant Harrison took it out of his file and gave it to Neil. I continued speaking. 'Gentlemen, coffee will be served with refreshments in our restaurant, if you will please follow me.' I put my hand on Neil's shoulder. 'Why don't you go and visit your father?'

'Yes Trevor, that would be better than ringing him.'

I looked at my watch. 12 pm, that gives us plenty of time. Tiny Harrison said to me, 'What are you doing on Saturday?'

'Nothing planned at the moment.'

'We are having an installation, if you would be interested.'

'Yes, I would.'

'I'll have a car pick you up at 10 am. Dress is dinner suit, black bow tie. I will have a Masters Apron ready for you.'

'Thank you, Tiny.'

'You have potential, Trevor; we need members. Now, where's the bar?'

The government car picked us up at 3.15 pm and delivered us to our next meeting. We all sat around the conference table. Fussy sat next to Michelle. I sat on the other side of Michelle. Sir John Moore sat opposite us, with two other gentlemen. Frank sat next to Bill. I whispered to Michelle. 'It's all yours. Play the game.'

Sir John said, 'Ladies and gentlemen, my superiors are very pleased with the outcome of our meeting yesterday, and the Prime Minister has signed the documents. I will sign, and my witness will sign.' He took his pen out of his top pocket and signed the document; the other two gentlemen did the same. He gave the documents to me with his pen. I looked at Michelle and said, 'Sign.'

She took the pen and papers and signed them, then I signed the papers using the same pen. Bill co-signed as the lawyer and then he passed the papers to Fussy. She looked and hesitated. Michelle pointed to the paper and where to sign, and she signed.

I said to Sir John, 'This lady was one of Peter Smith's most trusted employees.'

A lady came in with what appeared to be a red candlestick. Sir John rolled up the document and sealed it with the red wax; then he pressed the seal into it. And the lady walked back out with the seal.

Sir John said, 'This land now belongs to the Square Mile of London, and these documents will now go into the archives in the Tower of London.' That took me totally by surprise. He then said, 'You have taken care of one lawyer; we will take care of the other two.' He looked at me seriously and bowed his head. 'Trevor and Michelle, I think this occasion needs a glass of champagne, please follow me.' As we went back to our office, I thought to myself, *who would believe I've just had a glass of champagne at #10 Downing Street.* I think I'll keep that to myself.

We arrived back at the office. Fussy couldn't contain herself, telling Chris how she had signed the documents, which were sealed with wax, rolled up and would go into the archives in the Tower of London and that she had drunk champagne at #10 Downing Street with the hob-nobs. She wanted to go home to tell her husband. In the blink of an eye, she had gone.

'Trevor, tomorrow afternoon you have a meeting with Lewis Constructions and the Airport management concerning the car park.'

'Thank you, Chris.' I looked at Frank. Should he be there tomorrow morning? If Michelle and Frank are going to marry, there shouldn't be any secrets. They hadn't mentioned marriage as yet, but they were going away for the long weekend. 'Frank, Bill, could you both be at the house first thing tomorrow, use the helicopter. Chris, could you also stay there tomorrow morning, and please let June know there will be two more for breakfast?'

Michelle was looking at me with a very suspicious look on her face. 'Trevor, what are you up to?'

I said, 'Come with me and see what's in my imagination. Have faith in me, Michelle. I've had enough for one day; we are going home.'

Before we left, I went to the safe and got out Peter's envelope addressed to me. All that was left in the safe was the money. I felt my job was nearly over.

When we got back to the house, I said to Joe, 'First thing in the morning, could you bring Bill and Frank to the house? I'll have a bacon and egg sandwich waiting for you.' He grinned at me; I winked back.

I walked into the house. June said nothing; she just handed me a bottle of Scotch. Grumpy told me you were coming; she had two glasses waiting. Grumpy and I sat quietly sipping our scotch. I took the envelope that Peter had left me from my inside pocket and handed it to Grumpy. He sat quietly reading through the contents. Then said, 'So, you believe she's ready?'

'Yes, I do. She also has two people to back her up. One will become her partner in life.'

'Does that mean I could become a great-granddad?'

'Grumpy, it's in the cards.' He gave the letter back to me.

'Trevor, on Sunday I have a party of five people coming aboard for lunch and a cruise up the river. Ernie and Win want me to do regular trips. The passengers will pay good money for the experience. I have a problem. Somebody has stolen my helmsman. Are you interested?'

'Yes, Michael, I am. My fee will be a plate of seafood. Where do you pick up your passengers?'

'London Bridge.' Just then, his mobile phone rang. 'It's June. Tea is ready. She's the only woman I jump for. Let's go.' Shirley appeared out of nowhere, wagging her tail. Michael said, 'Food.' Shirley jumped over the bulwarks onto the jetty and took off to the house. We followed.

CHAPTER 29

The next morning, we were sitting down for breakfast. Joe had had his bacon and egg sandwich, and Shirley was enjoying her breakfast. I sat there looking at everybody. Peter had such a large company, but the only ones I really met were these people. It has kept it simple for me, no fancy dinners, no wining or dining. I didn't have to go to any fashion shows or get tied up with other companies trying to use Peter's name to further their own companies. We eventually finished breakfast. June and Chris had done the dishes. Bill was looking at me. He had his serious face on. We looked into each other's eyes. He knew what I was about to do. I looked at Michael. The look on his face let me know that the responsibility I was now going to put on Michelle's shoulders, from now on, she will not be free; her grandfather's company will control her life. Two thousand people will rely on her. I thought you were sent here to do a job, now do it!

I heard myself speak. 'If everybody could follow me down to the computer room, please. Yes, Shirley, you too. Michelle, could you sit down at your computer? June, could you sit down next to Michelle? Frank, please sit down on the other side of Michelle. Bill and Michael stand behind her. Chris, will you stand behind June? Now, Michelle, open your computer, put in the password *Ready*.' I stepped back. Somehow, I knew what was going to happen. Michelle put in the password.

To everybody's total surprise a man was sitting at a desk. Standing alongside of him was Bill. The man at the desk looked tired and weary but he had a beautiful smile on his face.

He spoke. 'Yes, June it's me.' June burst out crying. Chris put her arms around her shoulders. Frank took Michelle's hand and squeezed it. Michelle kept staring at the man behind the desk.

'So, my beautiful granddaughter, you are now ready, and I can talk to you about the responsibility that you are going to take on. Bill has arranged everything to make it a smooth takeover for you, so don't worry. June, my darling June, I have put together a short video of our memories of the good times, but for now I must talk to Michelle and the rest of her team. June, go and have a cup of tea with Trevor, then come back and sit with me in private and we can go through the video together.'

Chris helped June up, and we went back to the kitchen. June and Chris looked like they were in shock seeing Peter on the video. I put the kettle on and made two cups of tea and one of coffee. We sat there quietly drinking them.

June looked at me with red swollen eyes. 'Trevor, you have completely puzzled me ever since you arrived. You say and do things the same as Peter. You seem to have the answers. You are like Peter, making everything a game. You say that you come from Australia, but you seem to come from somewhere else.'

'June, the only thing I can say is that I was born with a gift. It has got me into a lot of trouble over the years, but I know that I have helped many people. I am what you call a Medium. I get messages, but not always the answers. They flash through my mind — not the fantasy side, not the logical side but somewhere in the middle. I have studied it here in England; however, I believe I have been given a special job to do, and I believe it's now done. I'm almost ready to go home, but not quite yet.'

June stared at me, then went and got three glasses. She put Scotch in them and gave me one.

Then I said, 'I won't call him Grumpy anymore; he is Michael.'

She took the Scotch down to Michael and returned. We sat down and talked for a little while. Chris just listened. June wanted to know more about Mediumship.

'Yes June, there is more about life we do not understand. Everything is made up of energy, every living thing, the wind, the rain, the seasons, the sun and the moon. We do die but a part of our energy remains.'

June and Chris said nothing; they just nodded. They got up and started making some sandwiches.

'You like egg sandwiches, don't you Trevor?'

'Yes, I do.'

They put the sandwiches on the table and made tea and coffee for everybody. When they came back into the kitchen, they all sat down and quietly ate their sandwiches, saying nothing.

'Chris, will you stay here with June? She may need you for the computer and for support.'

'Yes, Trevor.'

'Now, we have a meeting to go to.'

We all got into the helicopter, and Michelle said to Joe, 'I'll fly and you land.'

Joe turned around and looked at me. 'Trevor, how do I argue? If I do, there will be no more egg and bacon sandwiches!' He raised his hands in the air. When we arrived at our building, Joe landed the helicopter, and once again Michelle studied what he was doing and how he did it.

The architect and the structural engineer were there waiting for us in the boardroom. I put my hand out to the first man. 'I am Trevor Evans.' I shook his hand.

'My name is Paul Smith, structural engineer for the airport and this is my colleague, Peter Conley.'

I shook his hand as well. Michelle introduced herself and shook their hands.

'This is Bill, the company lawyer.'

Three people were then ushered into the room, a lady and two gentlemen. The lady, who was smartly dressed, stepped forward and introduced herself. She was with airport management. One of the gentlemen did the same. The younger man politely nodded and said, 'I am here to observe, Sir.'

I studied him for a moment, there was something about him I liked. 'Your name, young man?'

'Henry Phillips, Sir.'

'You say you are with Airport Management. What exactly does that mean.'

'We are here to observe. When we return to the airport, we will write our reports and suggestions and speak to our consultants. At the next airport meeting we will present them.'

I looked at Michelle. Do I hand this over to her? She raised her eyebrows at me. No, this is mine. I looked at the lady in front of me.

'There seems to be a bit of a misunderstanding here. Airport management contacted us because they needed something from us. We came to an agreement. If we construct the building on our land, it belongs to us, not the airport. Airport management wants to lease it from us; therefore, we need a structural engineer from the airport and whoever looks after parking and drainage. I am sorry to say that you do not have these qualifications.'

I looked at Michelle. 'Do you have the telephone number of the man we first spoke to?'

She opened her file and rang the gentleman; she handed the phone to me.

'Good afternoon, my name is Trevor Evans, and this concerns the airport parking.'

'Yes Trevor, how can I help you?'

I explained the situation to him. There was a pause on the phone, then a sound, like somebody gritting their teeth. 'Trevor, there has been a misunderstanding here as well; could you put my people on?'

I handed the phone to the lady. She listened and put her head back slightly as though she were annoyed. Then she handed me back the phone. The man's voice sounded strong and in command. 'I will have the people you require there within half an hour.'

'Your helipad is free?' I asked.

'Yes, it is. I apologise for the misunderstanding. I wish I were working for you, Trevor, then I would only have to answer to one man, not committees.'

I handed the phone back to Michelle and looked at the younger man and then turned to the lady. 'Apparently, you're going back to the airport and the people I require are coming here by helicopter, but I would like to hang onto this young gentleman for his future training. I don't think your superiors would argue with that. Now on the next floor up there is a restaurant, please order coffees for us, just coffee, and you, young man return here.'

'I will show them,' Bill said, and they were gone.

The two men from Lewis Constructions were grinning. One of them said, 'That never used to happen in the past. Now it happens all the time, and it gets so frustrating, and time consuming.'

The other gentleman said, 'And it happens in our own office.'

They spread their paperwork out on the table. With my little knowledge I was very impressed, the architect hadn't wasted any space or put any unnecessary fancy work around the structure to make a statement for himself.

'I'm very grateful to you, Bill, you mentioned drainage when I rang the airport, I just got red tape, no answers. Now what we suggested for industrial waste, such as car washing, is that we have put in a metre wide tank down the fence line, three metres deep, so it should take up less space for transport parking, nothing would be parked on top of it.'

We talked for a while, and then the young man returned. The three gentlemen from the airport came in, and we introduced ourselves. They nodded briefly to the young man, obviously knowing who he was. 'Now, gentlemen, could I hand this discussion over to Michelle?'

She nudged me with her shoulder and grinned at me. She looked at the young man. 'Young man put this into your book of learning. He has just passed the buck to me. Now we have been discussing drainage, which is obviously your expertise, it has been suggest by Lewis Construction to put the industrial waste tank down the fence line, 3 metres wide, 3 metres deep and 20 metres in length.' He looked a little startled but did not hesitate.

'Yes gentlemen, I think that is very practical, and a lot easier to clean, and you wouldn't miss that space.'

The drainage man from the airport said, 'I agree with that.'

I nodded to Bill and gestured to the door, and we both left.

'Coffee, Bill?' I asked as he pushed the button on the lift to the top floor.

We chatted for a while, then eventually Bill said, 'Do you think we had better go back down?'

'Yes,' I replied.

We went back into the Conference room and discreetly sat down, listening to the talk with the young man joining in with very practical suggestions. Bill leaned over to me and quietly said, 'I don't think they missed us!'

The gentleman from Lewis Constructions said, 'Well Michelle and gentlemen, I think we've covered everything, and this discussion on the project has made things a lot simpler.' He looked at Michelle, then me. 'Are you ready to sign so that the project can go ahead?'

'Would you like to sign first?' Michelle whispered to me.

'Michelle, I think Bill would agree with me, you should sign it first.'

'Are you passing the buck again, Trevor?'

I breathed in heavily, then breathed out again. 'Yes, Ms Smith.'

The two gentlemen from Lewis Construction looked confused. Michelle said to them, 'You have both been here to witness a very big day in my life.' She paused for a moment. 'My grandfather's company has officially been handed over to me.'

She signed the papers, and then Bill signed. Then he said to the young man, 'Could you please sign this as a witness?' He did, and everything was set in motion.

I said to Michelle, 'Could you get me that man from the airport on the phone again, please?'

She did and passed the phone over to me.

'Yes, it's Trevor Evans here. Our meeting has gone extremely well, and we have now signed the papers for the building to be built. Yes, your people have done a marvellous job, including the young man who is here. I'm sure you are obviously training him for something a lot higher. Could I suggest you involve him in the building of the carpark? He has a fresh mind, and he's very practical. I think that could serve both of us well. I will leave that with you and thank you.' We both hung up.

'Michelle, I think you owe us all a drink.'

She shook her finger at Bill and me, and said, 'I think you two have set me up nicely and you say I owe you a drink. To the bar gentlemen.'

CHAPTER 30

Michelle landed the helicopter on the lawn at the house and shut everything down. She said to Joe, 'This is our helicopter; you can have it when I don't want to play with it. You wash, clean, refuel it and fill in the paperwork and I will make sure you get egg and bacon sandwiches.'

Just then, Shirley came bounding up from the steam yacht. We all made a fuss of her and went into the house. June handed me a bottle of Scotch. I thanked her and went down to see Michael.

The next morning, whilst sitting at the breakfast table, Michelle said to me, 'I have asked Pananda to be in the office at 9 am to officially welcome her to the company. Would you like to put her on a contract, Trevor?'

'You put people on contracts so that they cannot leave and cannot be poached by other companies; it is a good insurance policy. Your relationship with Pananda, how much faith do you have in her?'

'From my point of view, it is business. I would ask for a contract.'

'You could be tactful so as not to offend her, by giving her the choice.'

'Thank you, Trevor.'

'Michelle, what time are you playing with the helicopter?'

'Trevor, I don't have anybody sitting at the desk for Marketing and Sales. Business first, then I can play. Trevor, I am now big bossy, I can do anything I want, can't I?'

'Yes, Michelle, but only if you play the politics correctly. You are now playing games with one hand tied behind your back. The company comes first; you are second.'

'Well, Trevor, Shirley comes with us today. Granny, Granddad and I have decided Shirley stays with us. If Shirley isn't home, then my uncle cannot take her.'

I put my hand up to my chin and rubbed it. 'Nothing to do with me, Michelle. I'm just an observer. Take Shirley for a walk around the garden before you leave.'

I gave Joe his egg and bacon sandwich. Then, Shirley and I got into the back of the helicopter. Shirley just jumped in with no problems, logic. It is just like a car.

Once again, Michelle studied Joe and the way he landed the helicopter. She said to Shirley, 'I'm sorry, but you need to have your lead on.'

Pananda was in the office waiting for us. 'Good morning, Pananda. Coffee for four, please, Fussy.' Shirley sat next to Chris; she was quite happy.

Frank walked into the office. 'Fussy, make that five coffees, please.'

Michelle sat down at her desk and patted her new computer. Frank said, 'I've got one of them too, and Ronald will be in later to show me all about it.'

'To business,' Michelle said. 'Mrs Pananda Kolhman, I would like to officially welcome you to the company as Sales and Marketing Manager. On these documents are your entitlements with your salary to be paid monthly.' Michelle gave Pananda the documents. 'Please read through these.'

Fussy brought in the coffees.

'You look after your staff extremely well. Can I choose the car?' Pananda asked.

'Yes.'

'I would like one more thing,' Pananda said.

Michelle folded her arms and leaned forward on her desk. 'What would that be?'

Pananda grinned and said, 'Fussy.'

'No, because she's part of the furniture,' Michelle answered.

Pananda then said, 'I would be very pleased to accept this position on these terms.'

'One more thing,' Michelle said. 'You and I have been friends since university. I don't want to lose you as a friend, but this is business. All of our top management is on a contract. What are your thoughts?'

'Michelle, I now work for you. If I did not sign a contract, it wouldn't go down well with the rest of your management team, so with respect to you, I will sign a contract.'

Frank slipped the contract over to her. She signed all the paperwork. We all shook hands with her, and Frank said, 'Welcome aboard. I've got a man you might know to show you how to work your new computer; it will be linked up to ours. If you would like to drink your coffee, I will introduce you to everyone in your department, and Michelle will see you later. She has a gentleman waiting for her.'

Michelle looked down at Shirley and told her to stay with Chris. 'If you have a problem, Chris will take you for a walk.' She smiled at Chris and headed for the door, saying 'bye bye.' She was gone.

Chris told me, 'There's a gentleman on the phone for you, Trevor. He is the manager of the construction site next door.'

I took the phone. 'Trevor Evans here.'

'John Simmons here. Yes, Trevor, the same one.'

'John, you certainly get around. How are your wife and children?'

'They want to go back to Australia to go camping in the bush again.'

'How can I help you?'

'Three days ago, an engineer turned up from Dubai. He doesn't understand that he cannot talk to the workforce the same as he does in Dubai, and now, I've got the union on my back. Can you help me?'

'I will make a phone call, John.'

'Chris, could you get me Ali from Dubai on the phone, please? Yes, the private number.'

I picked up the phone. 'Yes, Ali, I have a problem. John Simmons, Managing Engineer on your site, has a problem with a young engineer from Dubai. He doesn't understand the workforce here and has upset them, and now John has union problems. Can you help him?'

'Do you think he needs to be transferred back to Dubai?' Ali asked.

'Yes, Ali.'

'Consider it done.' He hung up.

We could hear the helicopter landing and taking off. They were really putting Michelle through her paces. I rang John back. 'The man in question will be re-located back to Dubai. Anytime I can help John, but I'll be heading home soon.' I hung up.

Michelle came back into the office; she didn't look happy.

'What's wrong, Michelle?'

'I got my helicopter license signed, now I can land on top of the building. The officer made me sweat to get my license. He knew how to play the power game, and Joe, our pilot, found it very amusing. He had trouble keeping it to himself.'

Just then, Neil Gilham knocked on the door and looked into the office. 'May I talk to you please, Trevor?'

'Neil, I was just about to take Michelle up for lunch; would you care to join us?'

We sat at a table next to the window and ordered drinks and lunch. I looked at Neil; he looked different somehow, more relaxed. His nervousness had gone, but then I thought, so had Naomi. 'You have a problem?' I asked him.

'Yes, my father wants me to go back and work for him and to prepare myself to take over his position. My contract expires in another two months.'

'Would you have any suggestions as to who could replace you?' Michelle asked.

'Yes, my secretary, Joyce Hollingsworth. She is British and has lived most of her life in Australia. She was employed as a secretary to the Managing Director of the SEC in Melbourne, Australia. She is very loyal and very sharp and methodical. I could trust her 100%. She understood my predicament with my so-called wife and played it tactfully.'

'Could you have her meet me in my office in one hour?' Michelle asked.

We had our lunch, talked and listened to Neil, and he put the situation into perspective. Then we went back down to the office. Michelle rang Frank and told him about the situation. 'Could you be in my office in 15 minutes?'

Joyce and Neil came into the office. Michelle spoke to Joyce. 'Please sit down, Joyce.' Joyce sat down. Neil sat next to her. 'Neil has told us that his father needs him, so his position as General Manager will be vacant. Would you be interested in taking up his position within our organisation?' Just then, Frank walked in with a folder under his arm. He sat down.

Joyce replied to Michelle, 'Yes, Ms Smith, I would.'

'My name is Michelle. Call me Michelle. You are my right hand.' She winked at Frank. Joyce knew exactly what she meant and smiled.

Frank put the file in front of her and said, 'These are your entitlements, salary and your contract with this company. You only answer to Michelle.'

Joyce read through the papers and read them again. She appeared to be thinking carefully. When she had finished, she said, 'Yes, I would be delighted to be part of this organisation as General Manager. Now I will need a secretary. The young lady Jodie Howard, may I have her as my secretary? Her mind is fresh, not cluttered up with other people's thoughts and ideas. I can train her well. She is very switched on.'

'On Tuesday we will have lunch together with Neil and go over our thoughts and ideas for the future, and I will ask Pananda to join us as well, so that we are working together as a team. Our accountant, George, tells me the company is financially sound and doesn't owe anybody money. Everything is now in order. My next concern is in disposing of the two factories. They have been burning industrial waste at those factories. Now this is a long weekend, I think everybody wants to go home. Thank you for the meeting.'

I heard a small helicopter landing on the roof's helipad.

Michelle grinned, looked at me and said, 'Finish one game and start another. Are you ready, Frank?'

'Yes, Michelle, let's go.'

Michelle said, 'Goodbye everyone, have a wonderful long weekend.' And they were gone.

'Young love, they never even said goodbye to Shirley,' Chris said.

'Chris, could Shirley and I get a lift home with you, please?'

'Yes, of course, Trevor.'

Chris opened the passenger-side door for me. Shirley jumped in and sat down before I could get in. 'Trevor, Shirley normally sits in the front.'

'Okay, then, Chris, I will sit in the back, and you two women can chat.'

We got back to the house, and June handed me another bottle of Scotch. Shirley and I went down to the steam yacht to see Michael. We sat talking about the day's events and the new staff. Michael's phone rang, Shirley's ears pricked up. The next minute she was off to the house. Food. Michael and I followed her.

CHAPTER 31

Shirley and I woke up the next morning. Saturday, do I sleep in? No, I got up, opened the curtains and stood there admiring the garden. It was a perfect English garden. I went and had my shower; a dinner suit had been laid out on the bed with a white shirt and bow tie. Alongside there was a Masonic briefcase. I got dressed in my dinner suit, put my black shoes on, then opened the case. There was a Past Masters Apron inside. I went down for breakfast. 'June, you would never believe it. This suit and case just appeared out of nowhere.'

'Yes, Trevor, a Stephen Evans delivered them yesterday. He said he was from the Lodge and would pick you up at 11 am today.' June poured me out a glass of milk and topped it up with cream. 'Trevor, you are not a drinker; this will give your stomach lining.'

Stephen picked me up at 11 am sharp. I shook his hand. This young man impressed me very much. 'I am Stephen Evans. At the moment, I am the Master of the Lodge. It is the Lodge of London and is in Croydon.'

Stephen returned me home at 6 pm. I had thoroughly enjoyed myself; a good day was had by all. I slept very well that night.

June woke me at 6 am. Shirley just put her paws over her eyes and growled. 'Shirley, you are one spoilt dog!'

I had a shower and put on my grey trousers, white shirt and dark blue reefer jacket, which had impressive silver buttons. I had my breakfast, and Shirley had hers.

The whistle from the steam yacht blew three times, and June gave me that look. Then she said to Shirley, 'Yes, you are going too. I don't want you to be at home when he comes to pick you up. You are staying with me! Trevor, please take Shirley the long way down to the steam yacht so that she can use her bowels.'

I stood there for a moment looking at Lillie, the steam yacht. 'Lillie, you are beautiful.'

Michael was ready, and he gestured to the bow line. I let it go. Then I walked to the stern, untied the stern line, and climbed aboard, pulling the stern line in so that it didn't get tangled with the propeller. I waved to Michael, then we started to move forward. I liked the sound of the engine. Chug, chug, chug as we gently moved off and headed down to London.

We passed all the famous landmarks, like Windsor Castle, Greenwich, which is the centre of time. We steamed under Tower Bridge, past the Navel warships, then we tied up at a small wharf. Michael said, 'It's a lot easier at high tide; when we come back, it will be low tide. Now, where are our passengers? We are at our designated jetty at the correct time.'

Just then a tour bus arrived; six passengers got off the bus and boarded the steam yacht. I stood at the helm and Michael welcomed his passengers aboard. Judging by their accents, they were all American. Michael walked up alongside me, checked the steam gauge and said, 'She's all yours, Trevor.'

I smiled and did exactly what I had been instructed to do. We moved off, heading back up the Thames. Being at the helm of such a beautiful craft gave me a huge sense of pride.

As we steamed past the Tower of London, Michael gave a commentary of its history, and the people who had lost their lives there. A German spy became more famous because he was the last person to be executed at the Tower. Michael continued his commentary of the Tower Bridge and its history and of Greenwich and Windsor Castle. He pointed out various things and how they had been a part of British history.

We tied up at a small jetty on a slipway. Shirley appeared out of nowhere and jumped onto the jetty and went into some bushes. When she came out, she ran up to the pub. Ernie and Win came out carrying picnic baskets. Three young ladies dressed in nice clothes followed them down to the steam yacht. Michael and I took the baskets from them, and the three ladies came aboard.

'Shirley will be alright with us until you return,' Ernie said.

'We can't have a dog aboard while we're serving food,' Michael said to me. We headed up the river; I was back at the helm. The young ladies prepared the food. It was the same as we had before, except for a plate with seafood on it for me. Michael opened both red and white wines and served them to his passengers, who were enjoying the food. He continued doing his commentary on the beautiful houses we were passing, who lived there and their positions in society. I was thoroughly enjoying the day and my position at the helm and the beautiful English countryside.

'Trevor, if you pull slightly over to port, throttle back, now turn to starboard, the current of the Thames will pull your bow around, facing us down river.' I did that, and we were facing the right way to head home. The passengers all looked very content, sipping their wine and just picking at what was left on their plates, but their stomachs were full. We again pulled up at the jetty, and the waitresses got off. We handed back their baskets, and all the passengers said thank you. Shirley jumped back on board, and we headed back to London while the guests were still drinking their wine, and Michael continued his commentary. Once we got back to London, Michael said. 'Would you like me to take the helm?'

'I think that would be a wise move, Michael. We moored at the jetty. The jetty was on pontoons, which made it easier for the passengers to disembark. They all shook hands with Michael and told him what a wonderful day they'd had and how much they had enjoyed the meal and the beautiful steam yacht.'

One man said, 'Quality and luxury, I will certainly look forward to doing it again.' He looked down at the dog, saying. 'See you again, Shirley.' He waved as he went up the jetty.

'Trevor, do you want a permanent job as a helmsman?'

'Michael, I will give it some thought. I've had a wonderful day just being the helmsman on this beautiful vessel.'

'Ernie and Win want to do this every Wednesday; they made good money today from people with money, and it puts it in my pocket as well.' He looked down at Shirley. 'Yes, and food in your mouth as well. I will give June the leftover ham and meat, so I won't get into trouble for making you fat.' I was totally convinced that Shirley knew exactly what he meant. We tied up at the jetty and cleaned the vessel, washed the glasses and then went up to the house.

June said to Shirley, 'Somebody came to pick you up today, and I said you were very busy playing with Michael. Tomorrow Chris is going to visit her daughter, and she's going to take you for the day, so that you won't be here.'

Shirley looked at Michael. He put his hands in the air and said, 'I know nothing, I see nothing.'

June spoke. 'Trevor, I'm having guests for dinner tomorrow, and you are going to do a talk about Australia.'

I smiled at her and said, 'Yes, dear.'

After tea, I walked out into the garden and sat down on the seat. I could see the house and garden and Lillie tied up at her mooring on the Thames River. To me, it was like a beautiful painting that would forever stay in my mind. Shirley jumped up on the seat and lay down. She put her head on my leg. I slowly stroked her head. 'Thank you, Shirley, for looking after me and for being my companion. I know that I would have been lonely and lost without you, and you have really sensed that.'

Just then, June walked out of the house with two glasses in her hand. She walked over to us. She didn't say anything, but Shirley got off the seat, and June sat down alongside me. Shirley lay down on the grass and put her head on my foot. I took one glass from June. We sat there watching the light fade over the garden. After a while, June said. 'Peter and I sat here. It was our private time together. We didn't say much. Peter just held my hand.'

I reached out and took her hand in mine. I didn't look at her, but I knew the tears were there. 'Trevor, you've been like Peter. Through you, Peter has been here tidying up the loose ends for Michelle.'

'Yes, June, he gave me a job to do, and I believe it worked out well, but that has been my life. I can break it all up in my mind, small projects and some big ones. This one has now finished, and I can go back home to Australia, to Jackie, Charlie and my family. Thank you for looking after me. You've had everything laid out for me in the mornings. You left Shirley with me during the night so that I wouldn't be lonely. I thank you for making this perfect.'

June put her head on my shoulder. 'Trevor, Peter and I are so grateful to you for looking after our greatest treasure, Michelle. She will take Peter's legacy into the future. For me, Peter is still here, his company is still here, he is alive, and with me always.' She smiled at me. 'And Peter is with grumpy old Michael. Come into the house; it's getting cold, and I still have the dishes to do. Yes, yes, Shirley, I'll get you something to eat.' We walked back to the house holding hands, not saying a word; it had all been said.

CHAPTER 32

On Monday morning, I sat on the edge of my bed thinking. Australia, what do I talk about, the past Australia or the future Australia? A feeling came over me. Australia is a love, a passion, a love affair. One moment she takes you to the highest place where you are soaring on the clouds, and the next moment she drops you, letting you know it's all about survival and everybody is in the same boat. She shows you the rawness of nature, floods, fires and drought, and then she shows you her beauty, the golden rays of the sun on her mountains, her beautiful forests and wildlife. The Barrier Reef, how old is she, her people have lived here for thousands of years, they say the time before the time, before the time. I shook my head. 'Come on, Shirley, breakfast.'

How does a dog move so quickly? One word — food! As I walked up the hall, the word Australia, its Indigenous people, they belonged to her; they had been with her since the beginning of time and asked for nothing. We, yes, we white people just keep on taking.

Shirley and I had our breakfast.

Then Chris walked in the back door and said, 'Come on, Shirley, we're going in the car.' Shirley took off straight out the back door, leaving Chris standing there.

June said, 'Food and the car, that's all she wants. When will you be back, Chris?'

'About 6 pm, June.'

'I'm expecting somebody to turn up for their dog, but I'm going to keep her. She's happier here.'

'June, I will see you later. If I don't go now, Shirley will start barking.'

I asked June if there was anything I could do to help her. 'No, thank you; everything is in hand. The table has been set, and the food is cooking. All I have to do is pick some flowers from the garden and put them on the table.'

June handed me a cup of coffee. 'Trevor, why don't you sit outside in the garden and relax? This is your day to do nothing.'

I didn't argue. 'Yes, dear.' I went out and sat on the bench looking at the garden. A car drove up the driveway, and a young man got out. When you're in your eighties, a young man is about 40. He went through the back door as if he were family. I could hear muffled voices, then June's voice got a little louder. 'No, she is staying here; she needs a large garden. It's cruel to keep her in a city flat. Now go and see your father.'

The back door opened, and the young man started walking down towards the steam yacht. He glanced at me, and I nodded back at him. Michael and his son came walking back to the house. His son went to the car and drove off. Michael went into the kitchen, then I heard June laughing. I think she has won, so has Shirley.

Michael came back out of the kitchen, looked at me and said, 'Good morning, Trevor, is it too early for Scotch when you've just had a win?'

Michael, we need to celebrate. I followed him down to the steam yacht Lillie. We talked for a while, and then Michael's phone rang. Michael said, 'Yes, Madam, no Madam, straight away, Madam.' He closed his mobile phone. 'Come on, Trevor, she has commanded.'

Guests had started to arrive. They joked and laughed with Michael, and he introduced them to me. Then, we all sat down at the table. One particular man, who seemed to be in control, said, 'So, you are the mysterious Trevor. We know why Peter picked you; it's because you are Australian. You don't mess about; you just do it and get on with it. I was in the Air Force as a fighter pilot, and your Australian fighter pilots were good. They didn't hesitate; they just got stuck into the fight. They made us laugh, their personalities are so different from the British, our officers didn't know how to take it. They were so practical and spot on.'

His wife said to him, 'That's enough about the war dear, I know it's your favourite subject, but it's over. Now, Trevor, my name is Isabel. We've all been discussing going on a cruise ship to Australia. Where would you suggest we go?' I thought, these are money people.

'I would suggest flying to Singapore when the cruise ships are relocating for the seasons, then cruise to Perth, which is a beautiful city. It's very friendly; the people are relaxed and don't run around in circles as quickly as the people in Sydney do, and you would enjoy their tours. Next stop is Adelaide. It is a very relaxed place to live. Some of the best wineries are in South Australia. I have been told that the best way to see it is in a hot-air balloon.

'From there, you go around to Melbourne, missing Tasmania. You normally arrive in Port Phillip Bay just at daybreak. I would suggest you be up on deck because the scenery is absolutely marvellous. Once you enter the bay, you go up to Melbourne. I live three hours north of Melbourne. In Melbourne, you can book a tour to Phillip Island and see the fairy penguins and Seal Rock. There is a zoo, which only has Australian animals in it. Melbourne is a working city. It is growing very rapidly, with migrants coming into Australia to find work there. We're having trouble keeping up with the explosion of people, although it is said to be the most liveable city in Australia. Its many factories and warehouses provide employment.

'Then, head to Sydney. Do not miss the entrance to Sydney; it is so majestic, you can't get enough of it in your mind. It is also a fun city. Go and see the Sydney Harbour Bridge, which you can climb. It's like a big coat hanger. It's a pity the English designed it, but on the good side, it was built by Australians. Next stop, Brisbane. Brisbane is the beginning of the tropics, and it too is a bustling city. She is the closest to our big industrial mines, which are north of Brisbane. We have coal mines, diamond mines and many other minerals, but I will say our mining for iron can be found nearly all over Australia. You would need six months travelling around Australia to see it all and meet the people who produce the sheep and cattle, the dairy food, fruit, sugar cane, bananas and pineapples. You would need to see the Blue Mountains and Ayers Rock in central Australia, whose Aboriginal name is Uluru, now.

'I could keep on talking forever because I love Australia. Now, when you're going to book that cruise, choose yourself a spokesperson to get it going and talk to the travel agent. Who would like to be the spokesperson and travel guide?'

Beryl put her hand up. I said, 'That's a unanimous decision, Beryl. You have a lot of work to do.'

I looked at her husband and said, 'Yes, I'm Australian. Looks like you are going on a cruise, no messing about.'

He shook his head at me and said, 'What mess have you got us into now?' They all laughed. Everybody had a good day, and eventually they all went home. Michael and I helped June with the dishes. As she was putting the leftover meat onto a dish, she nearly tripped over Shirley, who was sitting by her side, looking at her with big pleading eyes.

'Yes, Shirley, I've got meat for you, but there won't be enough for Michael.'

Michael handed Shirley a tea towel. 'You can dry the dishes, Shirley, and to think I stood up for you today.' Michael winked at me and said, 'I'm going home.' He left, and Shirley didn't seem to care.

CHAPTER 33

I got up early the next morning; it was still dark outside; I showered and dressed. Shirley stood staring at me as though she knew what the day was going to bring forth.

'Yes, Shirley, it's nearly all finished.' I went down to the kitchen and as I pulled the chair back to sit down, I said to June. 'It was a good day yesterday; they are very nice people. I hope I didn't bore them.'

'No, you didn't, Trevor. The women have made up their minds. They're going on a cruise to Australia, and so am I. No, Shirley, you're staying with Michael and Michelle.'

I sat in the helicopter looking down at the countryside and London, feeling a little sad. I had enjoyed the game, but now it was over. As we landed, I could see the small two-seater helicopter on the pad. I didn't go to the office but went down to the foyer to have a look at the new restaurant. It was very busy; nearly all the tables were full. Customers were buying egg and bacon sandwiches and other takeaway food. I sat down at an empty table. This is where I first came in, looking up at a glass building.

A waitress said, 'Can I help you, Sir?'

'Yes, one flat white, two sugars please.'

The waitress brought my coffee and two doughnuts and sat down at the table. 'How are you, Lesley?' I asked.

'Tired and worn out but very pleased. In one morning, we have made so much money, and everybody seems to be buying food from our restaurant. I don't have any more creditors, and I'm free to run my restaurant as I wish. Thank you, Mr Evans. Now I must go; it is very busy.'

'Yes, I understand.'

Just then I noticed Jodie Howard in her wheelchair. She went up to the counter and ordered two egg and bacon sandwiches. She turned her wheelchair around and noticed me. 'Hello Mr Evans, thank you for my new position.'

'Jodie, it has been a pleasure, and you have earned it. We met in this foyer some days ago, and I'm extremely pleased with how you are going. I will always have the memory of you. Fly high, my little white dove, fly high.'

'I will, Sir.' And she was off to the lift.

I drank my coffee and ate my doughnuts, got up and walked over to the antique car display and looked at the glass display cabinet with Peter Smith. I bowed my head in respect and then headed for the lift.

I knocked on the door of the office and walked in. Michelle was sitting at a desk, her desk. Frank was sitting next to her, and they were playing with the new computer. They both stood up, and Michelle came to me holding out her left hand, which had a lovely new engagement ring on it. 'Does Grandma know?'

'Yes, I rang her this morning, and she is coming in with Chris. I rang Michael and told him as well.'

'Very wise move Michelle. Frank, I've been married for 58 years and have never regretted it. It is all give and take equally. We took our vows again on our Silver Anniversary, in the same church. Jackie had new vows for us, and this is what we said.

Hand in Marriage

Give me your hand when life is Gay
All Merriment, Song and Play
A sweet untroubled holiday
Give me your hand

Give me your hand when I get mad
Say things I wish I never had
And show you all of me that's bad
Give me your hand

Give me your hand in Sorrow and Pain
A comforting hand to ease the strain
To give me courage, strength again
Give me your hand

Give me your hand
I'll not decline
What e'er befall
To give you mine

Just then, June and Chris walked in with Shirley, who ran to Michelle and put her paws on Michelle's shoulders, licking her face. Michelle cuddled her and showed her left hand and said, 'Look what I've got, Shirley.'

Shirley put her head to one side, looking a little confused. Michelle then showed it to June, who cuddled her, with tears in her eyes.

'Michelle, could I arrange the wedding, please?'

'Yes, Granny.'

Michelle looked at Frank. He shrugged his shoulders. 'Yes, Michelle, we will be very busy running a company, and as we have discussed, we will be in the deep end for quite a while.'

I put my hand out and shook his. 'Welcome to the oldest club in the world; life now begins for you.'

Chris and Michelle were cuddling each other, tears flowing everywhere.

Bill walked in the door. He was looking at us all, very puzzled. Frank shouted out. 'Bill, I thought you were my friend, but the documents I signed.'

'Yes.'

'Before I read them, you would think that I would have learned by now, wouldn't you? But they aren't contracts; they are a prenuptial agreement between Michelle and me.'

'But you drew them up, Frank. Remember flying out from England, and I was jetlagged and sound asleep in the comfortable chair. You put my hand in warm water, and I nearly peed myself in front of Michelle, and I said, He who laughs last, laughs best.'

He burst out laughing. 'So, we are square now, buddy. Now we have business to attend to.' He took the paperwork out of his briefcase. 'I have asked Sir John Moore to witness these papers. He will be here shortly.'

'Michelle, could you give me the paperwork that Frank signed?'

She smiled at Bill. 'Yes, as long as you don't give them to Frank. When he signed them, he'd had a little to drink, and I had been quite nice to him, so I don't want him changing his mind.'

Bill smiled. 'Michelle, I will help you sink the hook in deeper.'

'Thanks, buddy,' Frank said.

Just then, Sir John was ushered through the door. 'Good morning, everybody. Bill, you mentioned a good lunch, you haven't forgotten, have you?'

'No, Sir John, a deal is a deal.'

'Good man.'

'Now, everybody,' Bill said, 'we will bring this meeting to order. Could you please all sit down? First of all, Ms Michelle Smith, could you please give me your prenuptial agreement, which your future husband, Mr Frank Mattea, has signed?'

Michelle did so. 'Mr Frank Mattea, in front of these witnesses, do you agree to these terms?'

Frank replied, 'I do.'

'Could you please step forward to the desk? The one that's already been signed belongs to you. This one that's now in front of you will go into the records. Could you please sign here and here?' He handed Frank the pen.

'Ms Michelle Smith, could you sign here and here?' She did so. Sir John Moore, could you sign as a witness?' He signed as well.

He put a dab of wax on the paper, then pressed his ring into it. It was his official seal for the government. 'Mrs Chris Ayres, Secretary, could you please sign here as a witness? Margaret Fussy, could you step forward and also sign as a witness?' Fussy came out of the kitchen. They all knew she had been standing at the door listening and watching. 'Could you please sign here, and here as a witness.' She did so, looking very pleased with herself before returning to the kitchen.

Bill put the documents in two envelopes and gave Frank his.

Bill said, 'The next item on the agenda is for the owner of this company, Mr Trevor Evans, to transfer his company to Miss Michelle Elizabeth Smith and Mrs June Margaret Smith, who will remain a silent partner. Could you please read through these documents?'

Sir John read through them. 'Yes, these are the documents that we had drawn up in the interest of the Crown, the company's employees and its customers, which this company provides housing for His Majesty's subjects. I, Sir John Moore, will witness the signing of these documents on behalf of the King and the British Government.'

Bill said, 'Mr Trevor Evans, do you willingly hand this company over to Ms Michelle Smith?'

'I do.'

'Then could you please sign here, and here.' I did so.

Sir John stepped forward and signed, also pressing his seal next to his signature.

'Mrs Christine Ayres, you are Trevor Evans' secretary, is that correct?'

'Yes, it is.'

'Could you also please sign here and here?' She did so. Bill signed his name twice, William Farquhar, Lawyer for the Company Peter Smith. Bill looked at Sir John. 'Is it legal for Frank Mattea to sign these documents as well?'

'Yes, they are not married yet.'

'Thank you, Sir John.' He handed Frank the pen. Frank signed his name under William Farquhar, also stating Lawyer for the Company.

'Mrs Chris Ayres, could you please get two photocopies of this document?' Chris did so.

Bill gave the original to Sir John, a copy to Michelle and one to me.

'Mrs Ayres, could you please ask the people outside the door to come in?' She nodded to Bill and did so. Neil Gilham came in the door and stopped. He ushered two ladies in before him. I smiled. The arrogance had gone. He had done the right thing for the ladies.

'Joyce Hollingsworth and Pananda Kolhman.' Bill politely said. 'Could you please sit down? While you have been waiting, the company has changed hands from Mr Trevor Evans to Ms Michelle Smith. So, Mr Neil Gilham, Mr Evans accepts your resignation, though not with regret. It gives him great satisfaction knowing that you will be working for your father and taking on great responsibilities. If you would sign these documents.'

Neil Gilham did so and shook my hand. He said to me, 'Thank you for showing me in a practical way my arrogance and bullying ways. You have taught me to be prepared for what is in store for the future. I am very grateful to you; you have been like a father.'

'Neil, Peter Smith would be very proud of you. You can now take the responsibility on your shoulders for your father.'

Bill sat up. 'I will now hand this over to Michelle Smith for you two ladies. I'll be working for her.'

Michelle stood up. 'Joyce Hollingsworth, you have agreed to take over this company as General Manager. I understand the responsibility I'm placing on your shoulders as I ask you to sign the documents that our lawyer has prepared.'

Bill said to Joyce. 'You have read your contract with this company, and you have agreed to it. Are there any other questions?'

Joyce said. 'I agree to it, and I know there will be questions in the future.'

'Then if you would sign here and here.' He handed her the pen; she signed. Sir John stepped forward as a witness and signed as well. Michelle shook hands with Joyce.

'Welcome aboard Joyce, you are my right hand. You will only answer to me and nobody else.' Then she said to Pananda Kolhman. 'Do you accept the position of Marketing Manager and Sales, and do you agree to the contract?'

Pananda said, 'I do.' She signed her contract.

'Pananda, my door is always open to you; you don't have to go through anybody else. To keep my manager happy, I expect both of you to work as a team with me. Now, ladies and gentlemen, we will have lunch, then we will return here and have our first meeting.'

Shirley turned up out of nowhere and sat down by Michelle. 'Shirley, I didn't say food, I said lunch, but you know the difference, don't you.'

Michelle looked at her grandmother. 'Michelle, I am a silent partner, and Shirley is family. She doesn't want to miss out on this special occasion.'

Bill put his hand on Chris's shoulder. 'Could you wait a moment, June? Could you stay with us for a moment?' After everybody left, he handed Chris a document.

'This gives you life tenancy for the cottage you're living in. June, the reason you are a silent partner is to protect your home and your lands. The company pays for your gardens, any repairs to the house, your bills, and they will pay you a retainer every month.' June looked at him with a serious look on her face.'

'Thank you, William. You are our key player in the company, but you didn't sign a contract today.'

'June, I signed a contract a long time ago when you and Peter took me in as a young man. My contract is for life. I belong to you, and you are a silent partner.'

June still looked serious. 'Bill, when it's not so busy, can we talk about my retainer and a few little trips overseas?'

Bill smiled. 'Yes, Madam, whenever you wish.'

He followed Chris, Fussy and June into the lift to the restaurant.

Shirley was sitting between Chris and June. She wasn't looking so happy about the lift. Dogs are not permitted in the restaurant, but that's not my problem now. I'm just a guest.

As we got out of the lift, Sue Williams was there with four other women. She said, 'Good morning, Dad.'

'Good morning. Sue, have you met these two ladies?'

'Yes, I have. I met Chris.'

'This lady is June Smith, one of the owners of this company. Mrs Smith, this is Sue Williams. She works for the gentleman from Dubai and is looking after their women while they're in London.'

June said, 'I'm very pleased to meet you, Sue. We have a steam yacht doing trips up and down the Thames. If you are interested, please talk to Chris.'

'Yes, I am very interested. I will talk to Chris later. Thank you for your suggestion. I have to be very tactful and careful about where I take the ladies. However, that certainly sounds like a good idea, thank you.'

As we were walking into the restaurant, Chris said to me. 'Sue Williams came into the office and asked me a few questions about her position. She had a few small queries. She told me how tactful she's got to be looking after the ladies from Dubai, their relations with their husbands and respecting the way of life in Dubai.'

We all had lunch. Everybody was talking about their new positions and what their portfolios would be in the future. I could only nod and say yes or no. I was no longer a part of it. I felt sad and just wanted to go home to Jackie and our dog Charlie. I wanted to see my family, including the great-grandchildren. I missed them. I needed Jackie, and I needed to cuddle my daughter Deanna and stir my son-in-law up. I wanted to know how my grandchildren and their partners were. There was a pain in me, but where? It is in my emotions. I don't belong here.

We went back down to the office. I sat down on one side, out of the way. Michelle was sitting at her desk. She looked very serious and in control.

'Welcome to our first official meeting. I look forward to working with all of you. Over the years, we must work as one team to be successful. Any time you wish to talk to me, I will be here for you. You are my team. The first thing on the agenda is to clean up loose ends, the two factories.'

Bill spoke first. 'Yes, I have spoken to our broker, and he informs me that the insurance company will take the responsibility of cleaning up the factories and disposing of the waste. He informs me that the insurance company will not argue as they need us. We don't need them. We have too much insured with them.'

Pananda said, 'Joyce and I have been looking through the paperwork for the parking at the airport. The factories are three and a half kilometres from the airport, we could offer those factories as long-term parking on the same lease as the car park.'

Frank said, 'It could work if we splashed a bit of paint around, made sure the toilets were clean, that the sprinkler system was working correctly and that there were new fire hoses and alarms.'

Michelle sat thinking, and everybody waited. The only thing that stayed on her mind was putting these details on the same lease that joins the two together, making it less complicated for our team and one insurance policy for the airport and ourselves.

'Yes, I agree with you. Frank, Joyce and Pananda, if you could take care of that problem, it would be in our best interest to talk to the gentleman.

'Not their floozies in the office,' I said.

'Joyce, the house that Neil Gilham lived in belongs to this company, do you require it?'

'No, thank you, I have a beautiful home. It is mine, and my late husband used to live there with me, and it's close to here.'

'Pananda, are you interested in the house?'

'Thank you for the offer, but we also have our own home, and my husband would not move anyway.'

'Pananda, I need your husband in my organisation. You now know how big it is. The world we're moving into is all now through computers. The wrong person using a computer can bring us down. I need a man like your husband. I know I would have to let him be free to work on his own and to only answer to me.'

'Yes, Michelle, I think he would accept under those conditions.'

I sat there listening. I'm no longer part of it. My part has finished, but what did I really do? Had Peter Smith already had things in motion and had I just been a pawn in the chess game? I was sitting here, but I felt like I was invisible. The meeting finished, everybody left. I walked over to Chris.

'Chris, could you book me a flight back to Australia tomorrow if possible?'

She looked at me with sadness in her eyes. 'Yes, Trevor, I perfectly understand.'

I went and made myself a cup of coffee and sipped it, whilst looking down at the construction site. How it had grown since I arrived — nothing stays still. Yesterday is gone; tomorrow is yet to come; everything has moved on. Somebody once said to me. *You arrive in somebody's pain, and you leave in your own pain.* Is that in your body or is it in your mind? Now I'm getting sad because it is all over.

Chris said, '10.30am tomorrow?'

'Yes, Chris, that would be fine.'

'Trevor, could I drive you to the airport, please?' I turned around and looked at her. 'Yes, Chris, I would appreciate that.'

'I think June would like to come with us as well, Trevor.'

CHAPTER 34

I woke up in the morning. Shirley was still lying alongside me. She rolled over and put a paw on my chest. 'Yes, Shirley, you understand, don't you?' My emotions are caught between leaving here and going home. 'You have looked after me, you have understood my loneliness and laid down alongside me. You will stay in my mind forever.' I stayed there slowly stroking and petting her, but I didn't have any time to spare, so I got up, showered, put on the clothes I had arrived in and went down to the kitchen. I sat down at the breakfast table. June put my breakfast in front of me. She put her arm around my shoulder and her head on mine, and she started to cry.

'How do I thank you, Trevor?'

'You already have June, in the way that you have looked after me. My clothes have always been laid out for me, my breakfast always ready. I have wanted for nothing. You have made your home mine. I have played my part in the greater chess game, and Peter has won. Everything is as it should be, and June, you now have Shirley.' Shirley stopped eating her breakfast and looked up at both of us. 'Don't look at us like that; you're wiser and more intelligent than we are.'

All four of us arrived at the airport. The air was cold; winter had arrived. June said to Shirley, 'You stay in the car and look after it.'

I put my head onto Shirley's and said goodbye. I stroked her. 'Thank you, Shirley.'

We walked into the foyer. My bag was on a trolley. I put my arms around Chris. 'Thank you for looking after me, Chris.'

She put her arms around me and cuddled me back. I know she had taken tissues out of her pocket. She opened her bag and took out a small Golliwog. 'Take this to remind you of me.'

I took it and put it in my inside pocket. I turned around and cuddled June. 'Enjoy the wedding, June, and enjoy your cruise to Australia.'

I stood looking at both of them, then turned and walked over to the counter. I put my papers on the counter, then went through customs and boarded the aircraft. I took my seat next to a window. The plane took off and turned slightly to the left. I could see London below, then we were in the clouds. I felt weary and tired. I put the footrest up and closed my eyes. I seemed to drift off into a deep sleep.

Then I felt somebody poking me on my left shoulder. I tried to open my eyes but had trouble. They felt like they were stuck. Somebody still kept shaking and poking me. I opened my eyes slightly. It felt like I had sand in them, but I could see Jackie standing on my right side and my daughter Deanna standing on my left side. There was a man standing at the foot of the bed. He had a stethoscope around his shoulders. Jackie was squeezing my hand; Deanna was squeezing the other. I looked around, and I could see a heart monitor with all of its squiggly lines and other monitors as well. Had I had another stroke and survived? I looked in Jackie's eyes; I knew I was crying. Where have I been? Has it all been a dream? His life, but a dream, all a dream?

I stayed at Monash Hospital for another four days. When Jackie visited me, she told me, 'You were sitting in your armchair talking to me. I answered back, but you said nothing. You slumped over the arm of your chair. I realised you'd had another stroke and rang the paramedics. They rang the front doorbell, and I let them both in. You were flown straight through to Monash Hospital.'

'Jackie, I had the most fantastic dream. It was so vivid in my mind. When I get home, I'll tell you all about it. I thoroughly enjoyed the dream. I've never had a dream like it before.' I squeezed her hand.

'So far, I have had two strokes, and I've survived. But in my dream, I really missed you and I was lonely, so lonely. I wanted you to be there.' I squeezed her hand again.

When I finally got home and was sitting in my armchair, the whole family came to visit me. My two great-grandchildren were standing on either side of me. Daisy said, 'Pop, Pop, can I have the little Golliwog?'

I froze. 'What little Golliwog?'

Jackie said. 'I decided to get your suits dry cleaned while you were in hospital, and it was in the inside pocket of one.'

I stared at Jackie, and thought *No, it was just a dream, just a dream. Or was it?*

THE END, BUT OF WHAT?